Unchained

Nicole McGill

This is a work of fiction. Names, characters, businesses, places, events and incidents are either the products of the author's imagination or used in a fictitious manner. Any resemblance to actual persons, living or dead, or actual events is purely coincidental.

ISBN-13:
978-1545068076

ISBN-10:
1545068070

I would like to dedicated this book to everyone out there who fights day and night to be a part of the rescue world.

I would also like to give a special dedication to my Uncle Curt, who has always supported and encouraged me to write since I was a young girl.

CHAPTER 1

It was uncommonly cold for a mid-January night in Georgia, by far the coldest I had noticed since moving here a little over two years ago. I'm not talking about the kind where you throw a sweatshirt on and are good to go. Tonight was definitely worthy of a coat, hat and gloves. Unfortunately, but not surprisingly, I had none of the above. The chill from the wind went straight through my black long sleeve shirt. Most people with any common sense were fast asleep at this hour and wouldn't know until morning when they saw the news that it reached a record breaking low. I however, noticed first hand. As a matter of fact, I noticed everything.

The eerie groaning of the trees as they bent back and forth under the power of the wind sent chills through my entire body as I blindly navigated my way through the starless night. I could feel my hands begin to tremble as I closed the distance between me and my destination. It wasn't from the temperature but more so what I was doing out in it. There was no turning back now though. I had been waiting for this opportunity for over a week and here it was staring me in the face.

My life hadn't always been this action packed, at least not this kind of action. I was born into an extremely wealthy family, whom also came from wealth. My name is Karen VanOlsen, and to say the least I have lived a very comfortable life. I drove a brand new Cadillac and had all the latest designer clothes. My jewelry alone was worth more than what most people made in a year. Whatever I wanted, I got. Not to mention, I attended an elite private school in southern California, which I was basically considered royalty at. My life was one big party, where the fun never stopped. I partied until the sun came up every single weekend, and spent the remainder of the week lounging along our private underground pool working on my tan. I only dated actors and models, often times trading them in when a better one came along. For being only twenty-five years old, I had life licked. Or so I thought.

Unfortunately, as they say, all good things must come to an end. I found that out the hard way the day my grandmother passed away. I had always been aware that I would get an inheritance from my grandparents, and since I was the only grandchild I knew it would be a large one. However, what I wasn't aware of was the stipulations that were attached to it. Apparently my grandma VanOlsen didn't approve of my care free lifestyle where everything was handed to me and work was just a four letter word in a dictionary. In the letter she left along with her will and all the money, she voiced her dissatisfaction of how her only grandchild never went to college and was freeloading off of other people's hard work. After clearly expressing her opinion on how I had thrown my life away, she went into detail on how exactly I would earn my inheritance. Long story short, I had to move out of California with very little money and start a life of my own somewhere else. My parents weren't allowed to give me my portion of the money until they felt I had found myself, whatever that meant, and would spend it wisely.

A month after her passing, I left my perfect life behind and moved to Atlanta. It was no southern Cali that was for sure, but my best friend Trish had moved there right out of high school to attend college to become a veterinarian. She was able to pull some strings and got me a receptionist position at the vet clinic she logged hours at for school, so at least that was a start. One, however, that I was in no way ready for. Apparently being on time was a thing in the real world. I didn't last more than a month before I got the 'this just isn't working' speech.

With one failed attempt at a job under my belt, I found myself with hardly any money left. I had to break my lease, loosing even more money that I didn't have, and move to the outskirts of the city where rent was cheaper. Somehow, I landed a job working at a dog shelter, making less money than the vet clinic paid. Afraid to get fired again, I actually made an attempt to keep this one.

It's been two years now and I've come to like my job, well most of the time that is. My life has changed substantially since I walked though those shelter doors for the first time. Which leads me to the mess I am in now…

I took one last glance toward the two houses that sat near the front of the property to be sure they were still dark. This wasn't my first time sneaking around the property, but for some reason tonight my heart raced slightly faster. Off in the distance, hidden in the cover of the woods, I could hear the unsettling noise of chains clinking together. I knew there were a lot of dogs back there, but had never gotten an exact count. They, however, weren't the reason I was here. Tonight my target was closer to the house, making it all the more nerve wracking.

Lightly tiptoeing along the brush line, I made my way toward the back porch attached to the more run down of the two houses. Careful to avoid anyone's attention, I kept to the shadows as much as possible. The last thing I needed was to send a dozen pit bulls into a barking frenzy, which would for sure blow my cover. Some people might consider what I was doing to be stealing, and I suppose they wouldn't be wrong. I didn't see it that way however. I knew what was going on here, and what they were doing with all those dogs wasn't exactly legal either. I was only aware of one dog having been adopted from the shelter I worked at, and I'm fairly sure they were not following the shelters guideline to providing a loving home.

Reina was a sweet energetic pup full of love, she didn't deserve to end up in a situation like this. To be honest, no dog did. I wished I could save them all, but I knew that wasn't possible. The bond I had formed with this little brown dog was the only reason I returned to this place. Not that I didn't want to take them all, but I was treading in some seriously dangerous water here. After hearing the story on how she ended up at the shelter, I made it my goal to get her to trust people again. It didn't take long before she was sleeping in my lap and following me around the play yard like my silent shadow. Knowing what her purpose was here at her new home, it made me sick to my stomach that I had gained her trust only to allow this to happen.

I had been watching this group of men for about a month now. No one seemed to know who they were or where they came from when I asked around town, which only spiked my curiosity more. Normal people didn't keep a dozen or more pit bulls chained up in the middle of the woods. To my knowledge there hadn't been any previous cases of dog fighting having been reported in the small suburban town of Litchworth. All the cases I'd heard of, or we received dogs from, happened in Atlanta. That however didn't mean this wasn't a new one popping up or a hide out for someone who had a little heat on them in the city.

As I drew closer I could hear soft whimpering coming from under the porch where I assumed they had her tied. Trying to keep her calm so the other dogs weren't alerted, I whispered her name as I approached the dilapidated porch. A flashlight would have come in handy but I didn't want to draw attention so I settled for the light glow my cell phones background offered. It wasn't until Reina squeezed between two boards and stepped toward me that I had wished there were no light at all. My stomach turned into a thousand knots at what I saw attached to the other end of the chain. Covered in dirt and dried blood, my Reina was beyond recognition. Cuts and puncture wounds covered her once perfect face and continued down her chest and legs. I hesitantly crouched down next to the cowering dog to get a better look. Part of her right ear was only being held on by a thin piece of skin. None of the blood was fresh and most of the injuries had already scabbed over. Not wanting to touch her battered body, I tried to lure her the rest of the way out from beneath the porch. Eyes that were once so trusting and full of love, now only held fear.

My heart sank as I softly talked to her, knowing she was right back to being the fearful dog she came into the shelter as. The leather collar around her neck looked to be about three sizes too big and rubbed mercilessly on the open wounds. A dog by the name of Brutus must have been the collars previous owner, as there was still a tarnished and dirty tag with his name on it. My guess was a lot of dogs had seen that collar, it was stiff from wear and over exposed sunlight. Whoever Brutus was, I highly doubted they had made the tag for him. Images of a healthy and happy dog proudly wearing this once brand new collar ran through my mind as I struggled with the rusted metal clasp.

"Almost got it," I reassured Reina, "then we're out of here." Finally, I got it to break loose and slipped the leash I had grabbed from home around her neck.

It wasn't until we were almost to the road that I allowed myself to glance back to make sure we weren't being trailed. Seeing only an empty field I finally took a much-needed breath. Now I only needed to make it a little further without getting caught, and my second rescue would be a success. The fact that I only lived up the road a quarter mile proved to be rather convenient. Being the neighbor to what I suspected to be a group of dog fighters had its downfalls however. I could hardly keep a bunch of stolen dogs that close without getting caught.

Reina made number four on my stolen dog list. Technically I didn't steal the first two, they wandered into my yard a few weeks ago. Since neither had a collar on, I figured they had slipped them and gotten themselves lost. It wasn't until I discovered all the scars on their bodies that I realized they probably ran away on purpose. That night as I drove around looking for any indication to where they had come from, I stumbled across two young men who watched me drive by a little too suspiciously. I hadn't been aware that anyone had moved into the old houses until that day, but then again I rarely drove past them as my route to work took me the opposite way. The next night I walked the woods line that connected our properties, trying to get a better idea of what was going on there. It was then that I stumbled into the middle of a mass of sleeping pit bulls. It was just starting to get dark, to the point where I couldn't make out how many were there. All I could see were dogs tied up everywhere, just out of reach of one another. The only shelter they had was a bunch of plastic tunnels.

It goes without saying, the two wandering dogs never got returned. Instead, I went back a few nights later and took another.

Hoping to avoid tipping the owners off, I intentionally left the collar attached to the chain to make it appear as though he had slipped it like the others. Even though he was chained away from the rest of the dogs, further back in the woods, his excited barking stirred the rest of them to life. I only stuck around long enough to see one of the houses lights turn on before rushing deeper into the woods to avoid any confrontation. The dogs must have barked like that often as I never heard anyone coming after me the whole trek home.

After gently placing Reina on the passenger seat, I scurried into my old beat up car and made my way towards town. I was hardly a suspect for dog napping, standing at just an inch over five foot and weighing a hundred pounds, I was just the pretty little blonde that lived with her two mutts next door. No husband, boyfriend or any visitors for that matter, made me the least likely candidate if they ever came looking. I planned to stay off their radar for as long as possible, so a few weeks ago, right after the two female pits wandered into my yard, I took out a loan with the help of Trish, and bought an old rundown warehouse on the other side of town.

All I had wanted was to come home every day after work and relax with my two dogs. Somewhere along the line plans changed and here I was now, worn out and exhausted beyond belief, and on my way with yet another dog to add to my growing pack. Not exactly how I had envisioned my life two years ago when I left California, come to think of it I hadn't even thought of why I moved in quite some time. Having grown accustomed to this ordinary way of life, I occasionally forgot that every day that passed drew me closer to becoming a very wealthy woman.

The roads were empty at this time of night, making it look like a ghost town. It wasn't long before I pulled up next to the building that housed all my stowaways. Quietly closing my car door to avoid alerting the dogs, I left Reina where she lay sleeping and made my way inside to set up a kennel.

"Hey guys," I announced as I opened the main entrance door to the kennel. The building had several large rooms in it and right now I had all the kennels set up in this one. The rest were still cluttered with miscellaneous garbage left from the previous owner.

Several half-asleep sets of eyes peered curiously at me from behind their chain link fences. It wasn't often that I made middle of the night appearances here, so their confused looks and whimpers weren't a surprise. Greeting each dog as I made my way to the back of the room, I grabbed a few blankets out of the closet to put in the only empty kennel I had left. At this rate I figured I should probably consider picking up a few more. Between the dogs I had rescued off the neighbor's property and the few I had adopted off death row, I was up to eight now. That didn't include my 2 that lived with me either.

Every Friday the shelter had to euthanize to make room for the next week's intake of dogs. Recently, between having low intake numbers and a slight rise in adoptions, we haven't had to put any of the dogs to sleep. That wasn't always the case however, and more often than not I would bring home the death row dogs. The ones I adopted had nothing wrong with them, time just wasn't in their favor. I figured it wouldn't take much to find them homes, all they needed was the extra time. Thankfully we weren't anywhere near as high kill as the other shelters in Atlanta, or I feared I would end up with more dogs than I could handle.

Two of my death row rescues I ended up keeping as my own. Posh, a once forgotten about outdoor beagle, was now my constant shadow and the stealer of my pillow. He had the funniest personality out of any of the other dogs I had met in the past two years. Then there was Ace, my overly energetic husky mix who couldn't keep out of trouble. She was surrendered to the shelter by her owners, along with the all too common excuse of how they just didn't have the time for her. I wished I could take all the dogs home with me instead of keeping them in the kennel, but the landlord I rented from had a strict two dog maximum in the agreement.

Once the kennel was all set up, I fetched the still sleeping Reina from my car. Watching every exhausted step she took to keep up with me, I bent down and scooped her frail body up in my arms and carried her the rest of the way to the building. The moment we walked through the door, the entire kennel turned into a mad house. Dogs bounced off the fencing while barking frantically, just as they did in the shelter. I could feel Reina stiffen up the moment she heard them. My once social butterfly of a dog was now terrified at the sound of them. She buried her face into my neck as we hastily made our way through the row of kennels.

"Hush!" I whispered, as we past the last few dogs. I may have grown used to the chaos of a kennel, but that didn't mean the rest of the neighborhood had. We weren't necessarily in the heart of town, but it was still a residential area and the last thing I needed was complaints from the neighbors.

As soon as I had Reina in her bed, I grabbed a box of treats and began passing them out to all the dogs, hoping it would quiet them down. Everyone, with the exception of Jaxx, happily took their cookie to their beds and lost interest in the new intruder. Continuing to stand at his gate growling, Jaxx remained completely oblivious to the treat I was waving in front of him. He was a beast of a dog, by far the biggest pit bull I had ever seen. He was also the other dog I had stolen off the neighbor's property. The fact that he was ridiculously muscular and lacked the scars the rest of the dogs had, I gathered him to be a winner. Which would also explain his aggression toward any dog that came into his line of vision. There was no way this dog wasn't being used as a fighting dog.

"How am I ever going to find you a home?" I sweetly murmured to the frantic black and white dog. Dropping the cookie in his kennel, I left him to do his thing. There was no reasoning with him when he was in this state of mind.

Once all the dogs were finally calmed down, I returned to check Reina over now that I could actually see. Her ear would definitely need stitches, but that looked to be the worst of the injuries. Most of the scratches and tears were just surface wounds. Fortunately nothing seemed to be very deep and would heal on its own. After cleaning her up with a wet towel, I liberally applied some antibacterial cream. She didn't appear to need immediate vet care so

I decided to wait until morning and have Trish come look her over after work. She might only be a student, but her five years of schooling was already proving to be extremely helpful with my little rescue operation I had going on.

I stayed another hour or so longer to be sure Reina was settled in and comfortable before making my way home. At least I would get a few hours of sleep before work. I hadn't realize just how exhausted I was until I was half way home and began nodding off at the wheel. Between the heat I had blasting in my car and a sudden downward spiral coming from an adrenaline high, I wondered if I would be able to safely drive the last ten to fifteen minutes. To be safe, I cut the heat and rolled down my driver side window. The cold air hit my face like a thousand needles, but it did the trick. I wasn't an everyday smoker, but I lit a cigarette to help pass the time, which only resulted in a head rush. Work was going to be rough in the morning.

CHAPTER 2

As I had feared, work dragged all morning long. Between the pounding headache and burning eyes, I was miserable to say the least. I glanced at my watch and was disappointed to see only an hour had passed since I last looked at it.

"Karen, come help me with the new intakes," my boss yelled from the office.

More intakes when we were already near capacity was never a good thing. Unless we had a lot of adoptions, it wasn't looking like we would dodge the bullet again this week and would have to euthanize. Or rather, I would end up with more dogs. The idea of killing one dog to make room for another was just, unsettling, to me. I could understand when a dog was really sick or overly aggressive, not that it didn't break my heart just as much. However, the thought of doing it for space just seemed cruel. That wasn't my call though, I was just a caretaker. Thankfully we got paid this week so I would have the money to pick up a few more kennels before Friday.

My boss, Elaine, was a short stout woman in her forties. She had been a part of the shelter world for longer than I had been alive and knew everything there was to know about dogs. Without telling her too much, last week I brought up what I thought was going on at my neighbors. She didn't have too much to say other than telling me that without hard evidence of dog fighting, law enforcement wouldn't be able to do much about it. Apparently countless chained up pit bulls wouldn't be enough to go on. I left out the fact that I had recently confiscated two of them off their property. Elaine was a great woman but that didn't mean I fully trusted her. The only person who know about my extracurricular illegal activities was Trish. Seeing how she was my best friend and a vet student, I could hardly keep her out of the loop.

Upon entering the office, I was greeted by two overly friendly labs and yet another young pit bull. All three were strays picked up by our animal control officer. Once the mandatory stray hold was up, they would be available for adoption. With no stories or history to go on, it was harder to find them homes when people came asking questions. Everyone wanted an already house broke dog that was good with kids, cats and other dogs. Unfortunately, very few met all of the criteria everyone seemed to think made the perfect pet. At least with owner surrenders we had something to go on. The labs would go right away, with their happy go lucky temperament I didn't see them being here very long. The pit bull on the other hand, we had an abundant supply of and very few homes for.

Once all the dogs were settled in their kennels and the morning chores were finished, I met up with Elaine in the break room to take my short lunch.

"You're looking more wore out than usual," Elaine commented as I sat at the table across from where she was already eating. "All those boys your dating keeping you out all night?"

I had to chuckle at her exaggerated speculation. I don't recall how many times I'd been told that I was far too pretty to be working in some dirty old shelter. At first it went straight to my head, but the past year had somehow changed me. I used to be one of the most sought after girls back in high school. Having inherited my mom's green eyes and thick black hair, along with my dad's perfect smile, I never had any issues with confidence. I hadn't seen my natural hair since middle school however. One of my presents for going into high school, yes I got a party for that, was a trip to one of the best salon and spas in California. Not just anyone could turn black hair into a perfect platinum blonde, I found that out upon moving to Georgia. I was now rocking a more strawberry blonde tone since no one around here could get it right, especially on my budget.

"Dating?" I laughed." I haven't been on a date in over a year." The last guy I went on a few dates with turned out to be just like all the guys back home. Shallow, rude and self-absorbed. None of the qualities which turned me on anymore.

"Well maybe it's time you went on one again," she suggested, completely unaware of my lack of time or energy.

I watched her peel, or rather tear apart, the plastic wrap that covered the top of her microwaved meal. It was amazing how much this woman could eat.

"I don't have the time to date," I replied as I scooped up a spoonful of yogurt.

"I was only kidding," she affirmed between bites of what looked like some kind of lasagna. "You seem much happier now than when you first started. Whatever you're doing, keep doing it."

If only she knew that the whatever you're doing she referred to involved trespassing and theft. I wondered if she would suggest I kept doing that.

"Anyway, back to work. The Evans will be here shortly to look at Shelby and Tank," she informed me while dumping the demolished tray into the garbage can. "Hopefully one of these two will fit their perfect dog standards."

The Evans were regulars when it came to looking at adoptable dogs. Every couple of days they would call and ask if we had any new ones in that fit their criteria, then come and see them. It was no surprise when they left today, they left alone. They never agreed on anything, and always had something bad to say about the dog the other liked. There was absolutely no pleasing them and I was beginning to lose my patience with having to take time out of my already busy schedule to show them dogs I knew they wouldn't like. I feared if they did finally take one home, it would end up back here the next day.

Once my shift was finally over, I rushed home to let the girls out and feed them before heading to the warehouse to meet up with Trish. To my horror, as I was getting ready to leave I noticed two men walking in the woods behind my house. Recognizing one of them as the neighbor, I swiftly got back out of the car and began walking toward them.

"Can I help you?" I asked sweetly, fully aware of what they were looking for. Determined to keep up my cover, I flicked a lock of hair over my shoulder and flashed them the most charming smile I could muster. They needed to see me as the young, flirty, carefree neighbor who would never steal a dog.

"One of our dogs got loose last night," the older of the two men replied shortly. "Just looking to find her is all."

I had never seen them up close before, and was just now noticing how big and muscular they were. The younger one looked like he lived on steroids and did nothing but lift weights, although I doubted that was the case.

Keeping the distance between us, I took a few leery steps backwards as they approached. "Well I haven't seen any dogs around here," I answered, trying to keep my voice steady so they wouldn't realize how nervous them being near made me. "Hope you find your dog," I lied as I turned around and made a beeline for my house.

"Wait a minute," the younger guy yelled as he continued to close the space between us.

Great, I thought to myself, they know. I turned around and flashed another smile, "Yeah?"

The guy doing all the talking kept up his advance. "If you see any dogs around here, you be sure to bring them on over you hear?"

"Sure thing," I laughed casually, "I'm not home much so I don't think I'll be of any help. Sorry."

Deciding that was enough conversation with them for one day, I left the two guys standing there whether they were finished or not. Instead of leaving right away, I went back inside and patiently waited for them to disappear back into the woods. This time I took both my dogs with me as I went back out to the car. I didn't necessarily think they would be protective, but it did give me a little sense of security having Ace by my side. For being a husky she was unusually big, and I felt confident that anyone wanting to mess with me would think twice with her around. I didn't care for taking them to the kennel, but with the neighbors lurking around I didn't feel comfortable leaving them at the house alone either. I wasn't even sure how I felt about staying there anymore.

My girls were the first thing Trish noticed when she finally arrived. After explaining the run in I had with the neighbors she gave me the I told you this wasn't a good idea look I'd been getting a lot from her lately. She loved dogs just as much as I did, but was slightly more sensible.

"I don't think you should be staying at your house alone anymore," she began as we passed the dogs evening food out together. "Tell your landlord you need out of the lease then find somewhere else." Concern filled her abnormally pale face. Since the day we met back in middle school, her complexion never altered from that of a porcelain dolls. It went good with her dark hair though.

"I've recently started thinking the same thing," I admitted. "The loan payment on this warehouse has me pretty tight on money though. Not to mention the cost of taking care of all these dogs. I can't really afford to go anywhere else."

This got me yet another lecture on how she would help me if I ever needed money. I could hardly accept help from someone who worked as hard as she did just to put herself though school. Trish may had gone to the same private school, but her parents struggled to make that happen. They didn't come from money like my family. Both her parents worked countless hours to be able to afford the little they had.

Changing the subject, I pointed to Reina's kennel as we handed out the last two bowls of food. "Here she is," I smiled. There was something about the little brown dog that I just couldn't shake.

Pit bulls had never been my favorite breed, to be honest I was deathly afraid of them when I started working at the shelter. After the first month, however, that all changed. A dog named Rey came in, picked up one afternoon by animal control. They had found him wandering the streets after a good Samaritan had called and reported a small black pit roaming around the neighborhood. Supposedly, kids had been chasing him around throwing stones and whatever else they could find. He was one of the first dogs that I really bonded with. Even when no one else had showed him any kindness, he still wagged his tale and was adamant to give everyone kisses. Being new to the shelter world, after hearing his story I figured he would be mean toward everyone, and was surprised when I saw how loving he actually was. Elaine had told me about how pit bulls were some of the most forgiving dogs, but I didn't believe her until I met Rey. Later when Reina came in, I decided to name her after Rey since their stories were similar. Both were unwanted little pit bulls, rejected by everyone. One of the control officers gave Rey his name and explained that it meant king in Spanish, so when Reina showed up almost two years later, I chose to name her after the Spanish word queen.

Trish slipped a lead over Reina's head, careful not to brush up against any of the wounds, and led her into the other room where we had set up a table and wash tub. Not two minutes into her examination, she looked at me and shook her head. "This dog was definitely used as a bait dog."

"I figured that much," I replied. Gently stroking Reina's face, I waited for Trish to finish looking her over.

"This is your evidence Karen," Trish pointed out. "You can use her to prove that there are fighting dogs being held on that property and that might open an investigation. You need to take this to the police."

I thought about what she was saying and wished it were that easy. "What if there isn't enough evidence though? My cover would be blown and they would be extra cautious and I wouldn't be able to rescue any more of them."

"Don't tell me you plan on going back there!" she demanded.

Watching her dig through the medical bag she had brought along, I tried to come up with an answer that wouldn't end in me getting another lecture. "One beat up dog will not get them arrested and they're just going to keep doing this. All they have to do is make up an excuse how she got loose and one of the other dogs attacked her."

Holding Reina still, I watched my best friend clean her ear before adding a few stitches. It didn't look nearly as bad once all the dried blood was washed off. Only one of the wounds on her chest needed stitches as well, the rest would heal on their own.

Trish didn't say a word until she was completely done, and then I got the look. Apparently, my answer to her question hadn't gone unnoticed. "You're right," she began, "but what happens when you get caught? Do you really think they're going to be okay with you stealing all their dogs?"

"Of course they're not going to be okay with it," I laughed, trying to make light of the situation. "That's why I'm not planning on getting caught."

"Karen, I'm not kidding! You have to stop this before it's too late!" she replied angrily.

Trish had an unusually happy go lucky personality, so seeing her this mad was surprising. Careful of what I said, I explained to her what Elaine had told me. Without solid evidence like paraphernalia or a fighting ring, there would be no case. In the few trips I'd taken to their property I had never seen anything laying outside and I doubted they had a fighting ring in one of the single wide mobile homes. Most of the dogs were in overall good health except for the ones they used as bait. "I'm pretty sure they're just hiding out there and do the actual fighting somewhere else."

"That doesn't mean you should be sneaking around there, they could be dangerous," she finally replied, a little calmer. "I know you're not going to listen though, you've always been stubborn when you had your mind set on something."

I knew Trish wouldn't leave it alone, so I suggested we start cleaning the kennels and getting the dogs out for their walks. Having the routine down to a science, it didn't take long to get all the chores done. One would walk a dog while the other cleaned their kennel, and then we would rotate. It seemed to work really well and it allowed all the dogs to stretch their legs and get some fresh air. Jaxx was always left for last since he was a handful and required the both of us to walk him on double leads.

I put a slip lead on him and waited for Trish to grab another. "You've got to be a good boy tonight," I pleaded, as the pit paced anxiously around his kennel. I couldn't tell if he was happy being here or miserable sometimes. I thought being inside and off that heavy chain would change how crazy he was, but it didn't seem to be working. Late at night when the kennel was quiet, I would go sit with him and just talk. That seemed to be the only time he calmed down.

Trish returned a few minutes later and we led the dog through the warehouse together, trying our hardest to keep him in between us so he wouldn't fight with the other dogs as we passed by.

"I can't believe how strong he is," Trish muttered breathlessly as we finally made it outside.

"He had to be in order to carry around that chain he was attached to," I replied, remembering how heavy it was. "Who knows what else they made him do to build all that muscle."

Our walk went rather peacefully, but I was glad when we had him back in his kennel. It always made me nervous when we took him out of the building, you never knew if a neighbor's dog or a stray would come running up. Here in the south, there seemed to be no shortage of wandering dogs.

Trish left after checking on Reina one last time, leaving me there alone with a kennel full of sleepy dogs. I let myself in with Jaxx to sit with him until he was relaxed like I did almost every night. The anxious dog paced around for a few minutes and then laid down next to me on his blanket and put his head in my lap. I felt him let out a soft sign and begin to relax. For such a big, dangerous animal, he had just as equally large a soft side. I wished I could just curl up and sleep there next to him all night, but my girls were beginning to whine in the kennel across from me.

"Come on ladies," I whispered, letting the two dogs out. Sweetie, the pit bull that they were sharing a kennel with, tried to sneak out with them. The three got along so well, it was like they grew up together. I had contemplated taking her home with me numerous times, but the landlord specifically said no pit bulls allowed and I couldn't afford to get kicked out. I felt bad as I tried to push her back into the kennel and eventually caved. "Alright then," I laughed, "we will sleep in here with you tonight."

My sleeping arrangement wasn't nearly as comfortable as my bed at home, but at least I didn't have to worry about anyone sneaking around.

Work went fairly smooth most of the morning, apart from a volunteer letting one of the dogs loose. Thankfully all it took was a little baby talk and some treats to catch the escapee. Other than that, the day was unusually uneventful. I had just finished cleaning when Elaine called me to the office to do the last tour before we closed for the day.

Glad my shift was almost over, I tiredly approached the middle aged woman who sat patiently waiting on the bench across from the reception desk. "Are you looking for anything in particular?" I asked, trying to get a feel for what dogs might be best suited for her.

"A small pit bull," she replied flatly. After turning her bracelet around her wrist a few times, she finally looked up at me. "Did you hear me?"

"Yes, ma'am," I answered as politely as I could. Annoyed at her rudeness, I turned and led the way toward the kennel. "Well we have lots of pits here," I added.

Taking her to the group of kennels that held the dogs that had been here the longest, I hoped she would pick one from there. Seeing how they would be the first to get euthanized if space needed to be created, I always pushed them the most when adopters showed up.

"I said small," she sneered in the most annoying tone I had ever heard. "These ones are all too big."

Just the sound of her voice made me want to point her towards the exit. Instead, I bit my tongue and took her further down the line to where one of our new intakes was laying in the corner on her blanket. She was one of the prettiest pits I had ever seen, with almost an entirely white coat, the only markings she had was a brown patch on her chest. "This is Annie, she is one of the smallest pits we have right now. We found her tied to a dumpster last week, so she is a little nervous around new people."

"She'll do," the woman said, cutting me off before I could say how sweet and loving she was once she got to know you. Her voice lacked any sort of enthusiasm or excitement at getting a new dog. Typically, when someone came here to adopt they were overjoyed and couldn't wait to get the dog out. Not this lady, she couldn't have cared less.

Leaving me to get Annie out, she headed back towards the office. "Don't you at least want to meet her first?" I called after her. Either she didn't hear me or didn't care, because I didn't get so much as an over the shoulder glance before she disappeared behind the door.

I found her filling out the adoption papers we required of all our new adopters. "Here she is," I said, reluctantly handing her Annie's leash. Part of me was hesitant to let it go. Something about this woman didn't seem right, but there was nothing I could do if she was able to provide the information we required.

"You're all set!" chirped the office girl we had recently hired.

Helplessly, I watched as she pulled the scared dog toward the car. Even Annie seemed to sense something wasn't right.

"You have to provide a driver's license to adopt, right?" I asked the receptionist after they had driven off and were out of sight.

"Yeah, I think so," she replied, never taking her eyes off her phone.

"Can I see her paperwork?" Obviously she didn't hear me. "April! Can I see that lady's adoption form?"

The spaced-out brunette pointed toward the printer, where the paperwork sat waiting to be filed. This girl wasn't going to last here very long, I thought to myself.

Hoping to find something that would tell me who this woman was, I scanned through papers looking for an address. Relieved that it didn't match my neighbors, I jotted down some information and stuck the post it note in my pocket. I could probably get fired for violating some kind of privacy policy, but at this point I didn't care. Searching for something else to go on, I rummaged through the filing cabinet and pulled out Reina's adoption file. Laying the two next to each other, I looked for anything that might be a red flag. My heart stopped beating when I looked at the addresses. It may not have been the neighbors, but they both lived in the same apartment complex. This was no coincidence. The neighbors must be having these women do their dirty work.

Irritated, I rushed out of the office. "Tell Elaine I had to leave early," I sputtered at the teenage girl who was still fully engulfed in her phone.

It looked like I would be paying another visit to the neighbor's house sooner than planned. There was no way I was going to let Annie end up like Reina.

I didn't bother to go home, instead I headed straight for the warehouse. The urge to protect the dogs I already had was running high. Besides, my girls were already there and I could just stop for food on the way. Eventually I would have to go home for a change of clothes and to wash up, but that could wait until later. The thought of staying in an old abandoned building made me chuckle. I wasn't sure if I actually found it funny or if I was just delirious from a lack of sleep. If only my friends and family could see me now, they would never believe I was the same person. Truth is, not a single one of my friends bothered to call me since I moved out here, and my parents hadn't called in several months. For all they knew I was partying it up in Atlanta. I failed to mention that I had lost my job at the vet clinic, somehow I didn't think they would approve of me making just over minimum wage at some animal shelter. I definitely left out the part where I had to leave my nice down town apartment and move to the slums. The few sporadic phone calls I had gotten from them lasted only a few minutes each and I was pretty sure they were only calling to make sure I was still alive.

Trish showed up just as I finished passing out the evening feed, and we knocked out the cleaning and walking together in record time. Not once did I mention anything about Annie or what was going on for fear it would put her in a bad mood.

"Do you want to help me start clearing out one of the rooms?" I asked once we finished walking Jaxx. "I think I'm going to stay here again tonight."

"I don't have any other plans tonight," she replied sweetly, back to her old self. "You should call your landlord and tell him you want out of the lease. It would save you some money if you just stayed here."

I wasn't overly thrilled about the idea of staying here permanently, last night I got the worse night's sleep of my life. It did make sense, however. It was a lot closer to work, and would save me a lot of time not having to drive back and forth. The money I would be saving could also help a lot in making the warehouse look better and I could finally get an area set up for the dogs to play in.

"I think I'm going to give him a call tomorrow," I agreed as I led the way into one of the biggest rooms in the building. "Until then, we have our work cut out for us cleaning this place up."

Two hours later it looked as though we hadn't even begun. I didn't know who owned the building prior to me, but they were hoarders by the looks of it. Old pieces of furniture, desks, chairs, and an abundance of other odds and ends were strewn across the entire room. Of course, nothing looked in good enough shape to be worth any money and I would probably end up having to pay to get rid of it all.

We spent the majority of the evening moving all the clutter to one side of the room so it would be easier to remove once I had the money for a dumpster.

The entire time working next to Trish, I felt a pang of guilt for not telling her about Annie. Every chance she got, between her work and school schedule, she would come and volunteer at the shelter and help me get dogs out for walks. Over the past week she had grown particularly fond of Annie, and I didn't want to worry her with the information I had discovered earlier. Unable to hold it in any longer, I told her everything, and immediately regretted it when she began to cry.

"Why would they take her!" she choked between sobs. "She is so scared of everything, what good will she be!"

"I'm guessing they're going to use her as a bait dog like they did Reina," I answered sadly. "I'm going to get her though. Tomorrow night I'm going back over there."

"You can't go back already!" she exclaimed. "You were just there the other night, they're going to be watching. It's too risky!"

"I'm not going to let her end up like Reina. I'll be extra careful," I replied, trying to calm her down.

"Karen, just go to the police. Don't try to do this all by yourself you're going to end up in trouble," she sobbed.

"I need more evidence," I pointed out, surprised she wasn't more supportive of trying to get Annie back. "This is the last time I'll go there. After tomorrow night I'll go to the police."

"There's nothing I can do to stop you is there?" she asked, face full of concern.

"Don't worry about me," I replied confidently, "I've done this twice now and haven't got caught."

After a few more unsuccessful attempts to change my mind, Trish headed home for the night and I made my way to the makeshift bed we had set up in the now mostly cleared out room. At least it was more than I had last night, I thought to myself as I looked at the heap of blankets on the floor. Three sleepy dogs had already claimed the majority of it, so I settled for the little spot they left me in the corner and laid down for the night.

"Goodnight everyone," I whispered at the still asleep dogs.

CHAPTER 3

I could tell it was going to be a busy day the moment I pulled up to the shelter. Two cars were already there, with anxious families waiting inside them, even though we didn't technically open for another hour. Unsure if they were aware of the shelters adoption times, I politely filled them in before heading inside.

As soon as 9'oclock came around, one of the families that had been waiting came in to see the labs we had on stray hold. Despite the fact that they weren't available for adoption yet, it wasn't a bad thing to have a home ready and waiting if their owners didn't show up. It didn't take but a few minutes for the family to fall in love, especially the two young children. They didn't understand why they couldn't go home with them today and cried when they had to leave.

Before noon, three dogs had already found, what I hoped would be, their forever homes. It was rare to have this many adoptions in one week, but I wasn't complaining. I always enjoyed seeing dogs go home with their new families. It made all the hard work and heartbreak worth it.

Most of the time Elaine handled the adoptions while I did the cleaning and exercising, today however the chores got pushed to the backburner as we were both needed for giving tours and showing dogs.

"Karen!" I heard Elaine shout over the all the barking. "There's a gentleman in the lobby that I need you to help."

I had just started to get one of the dogs harnessed to go out for a quick walk, and had to leave the poor excited animal to go do another tour. It wasn't looking like many would be getting out for exercise today.

I put the harness pack on the hook and made my way to the office. Even though the guy I was supposed to be helping had his back to me, I could tell he must have been something special by the way April gave her full, undivided attention.

"I can take you on a tour of the kennel if you're ready," I announced as I walked over.

Aprils expression told me she was less than enthused about having her new friend taken away, and when the gentleman turned around I could see why. Tall, dark, and handsome didn't even begin to describe the way he looked. The first thing I noticed were his icy blue eyes, that sat between a perfect set of long, dark eyelashes. There was no way they were natural, I had never seen such an amazing color of blue in my life, and I had met a lot of blue eyed men in the time I had spent in Cali. His dark complexion and black hair had me guessing he had some Latino in him. In a world recently filled with only dogs, I had forgotten how attractive the opposite sex could be. Not that I was interested, or had the time for one, but a girl could still dream.

Slightly thrown off, I extended a nervous hand and introduced myself. "What brings you here today?" I asked shyly. As soon as the words left my mouth I realized how stupid I must have just sounded. "I suppose a dog."

"Yes ma'am," he replied, holding back a laugh.

I wanted to crawl in a hole and disappear.

"I'm looking to adopt another pit bull," he added.

A man, regardless of how attractive, was looking to adopt not just any dog, but specifically a pit. Instantly my guard went up. "What do you want it for?" I quickly asked.

Seeing his expression go from excited to confused, I immediately felt bad for jumping down his throat.

"I have one at home and was hoping to find him a friend," he replied at a loss for words. "I love the breed and would like another. Preferably one that's young and good with other dogs."

"Sorry," I apologized, feeling really bad. "It's just a lot of pits don't end up in good homes and are the most over looked dogs so having someone ask for that breed in particular threw me off."

"I understand," he smiled, apparently not to upset at my outburst.

"Let me show you what we have, and if there are any you want to meet I can get them out at the end of the tour," I smiled back. Still feeling bad for lashing out at someone who had done nothing to

33

deserve it, I led the way into the noisy kennel.

"I was hoping for one a little younger than what ya'll have," he began as we returned to the office.

"Well," I started, hoping I wouldn't regret what I was about to say, "I actually have one that you might like. She's still pretty young, definitely under a year old. I'm fostering her right now." That was a lie. I wasn't exactly fostering her, but then again I couldn't exactly tell him that she was stolen. Pulling up a picture of before she had been adopted out and turned into a bait dog, I handed him my phone to take a look.

"She is really pretty," he commented while handing my phone back. Our hands lightly touched, causing me to look away in embarrassment. Who had I become? The old me didn't get uncomfortable around men. I used to walk into a room and draw everyone's attention and not flinch. Boys were never an issue and now I barely touch one's hand and my stomach got all nervous. A guy like him was undoubtedly drowning in attention from women and used to it.

"I would love to bring my boy to meet her," he added, breaking the awkward silence.

"She isn't ready quite yet," I explained leaving out the minor detail that she was in recovery and possibly terrified of other dogs. "It will be a little while before she is ready to go to a new home. If you find another dog before then I'll understand."

"I really like her. Here is my number," he replied as he scribbled something onto a piece of paper he got from April. "Get ahold of me as soon as you can meet up."

This earned me a death glare from the irritated office girl, but I smiled and told him I would.

"It was nice meeting you Karen," he added before walking out the door.

The rest of the day was a blur. Dogs may be my life now, but I was still a girl, and he was really good looking. My interest level in men had plummeted since I began rescuing, and Eric, I learned the man's name to be, was the first connection I had felt toward anyone in a long time.

I couldn't let this new distraction cause me to lose focus however. Tonight was my night off and I planned on making another visit to rescue Annie. With how close my visits were becoming, I would have to be on my game and extra cautious.

It was nearly 10'oclock when I drove by the neighbor's house to see if there was any activity going on. It wouldn't be until way into the night that I paid my visit, but it didn't hurt to check it out beforehand. Seeing several cars in the driveway, my stomach began to knot as I drove past and headed for my house.

While waiting for the right time to make my move, I took a much-needed shower and then began to pack. I finally decided that I was going to permanently move into the warehouse and get out of this place. I didn't see myself staying here anymore and there was no point in paying for a place to store the very little that I owned.

Amazed that I was able to stay awake, by the time one in the morning rolled around I could hardly keep my eyes open. The minute the cold night air hit my face, however, my energy came flooding back.

I made it to the property line in what seemed like record time. I wasn't sure if this was due to the amount of adrenaline pumping though my veins, or the rain that unexpectedly began pouring down. Probably a little bit of both.

As I had suspected, I made out the shadow of a dog tied to the porch just as Reina had been. Hoping it was Annie, I crept as quietly as possible toward it. Flashbacks of Reina, coming out from under the porch in the horrendous shape she was in, began whirling around in my head. I only hoped I had come soon enough to spare Annie that same fate.

Relief flooded though me as I drew close enough to make out the shape she was in. It appeared that I had shown up just in time, as there wasn't a mark on her.

My hands shook as I struggled to unclasp the same collar that had held Reina captive. The wet metal latch kept slipping from my hands as the rain continued to pour down on us, causing Annie to grow more and more restless by the second.

"Shhh," I whispered to the excited dog, "You're gonna get us caught."

I had planned on using the same tactic I had the previous two times, leaving everything intact as though she had simply slipped the collar and wandered off. I wondered how many more times I could do this before they caught on.

None.

The answer to my question, was none.

Flood lights illuminated the back yard making it at bright as day. Quickly looking up as I finally got the latch open on the collar, I saw three men running towards me. I no more than got to my feet when it hit me.

I had never been shot before, and it hurt a whole lot more than I could have ever imagined. Not that I often thought of what it would feel like to be shot. Trying to push through the pain, I attempted to run for the woods but my leg had other plans, which landed me right back on the ground. Scrambling to get up again, before my feet were back under me one of the men tackled me. Laying with my face in the mud, I struggled to get out from under him.

"Get off of me! Let me go!" I yelled, still struggling to get up.

"That's not going to happen," growled the man I recognized as the one whom I'd talked to the other day. "Were you really stupid enough to think you could get away with stealing from us!?"

"I planned on it!" I hissed back, surprised that I wasn't crying from the pain.

"Give us our dogs back and we'll let you go," the man standing above us demanded. "One of those dogs you stole is worth more than your life!"

Yeah, I doubt that, I thought to myself. I wasn't about to tell that to them, however. I had a feeling I would be used as ransom if they knew the amount of wealth I came from.

In that moment, I wished I had told Trish where I was. She knew I was going to get Annie, but when she left after helping with chores earlier I didn't tell her it was going to be tonight. I didn't want her to worry. I knew she would eventually figure it out, especially when she showed up at the kennel in the morning and saw I wasn't there. The question was, how long did I have? As far as I knew, these people weren't convicted murderers. Just heartless dog fighters.

Two of the men led me toward the house while the other went off searching for Annie in the woods. It was a disaster inside and reeked of spoiled food. I looked around anxiously searching for a way out, only to find a girl passed out on one of the couches while another sat on the lounge playing on her phone. Lazily, she looked up when we entered the room and I immediately recognized her.

"What's up, shelter girl?" she sneered, obviously recognizing me as well. "Here to sell me another mutt and then try to steal it back? Is that how ya'll stay in business around there?"

I didn't feel the need to dignify her with an answer. Instead I looked away, focusing on anything but the sad excuse of a human that continued to stare smugly ahead at me.

"Sit here and shut up." The guy holding my arm shoved me into a chair and walked out of the room. "Find out where she's keeping our dogs!"

I remained silent, like I had been told to do, the entire time the girl questioned me. Focusing on anything but her, I realized I couldn't feel any pain from the gun shot.

"Maybe if we start killing dogs off one by one in front of you we will get some answers," she snarled, interrupting my thoughts. A smile crept across her face and I could only imagine the look of terror written across my own.

I still didn't say a word. She was bluffing. If the dogs really were worth as much as they claimed, there was no way they would kill them.

Irritated that her tactic didn't work, she yelled for one some guy named Rob to bring out the bait.

Bait? I thought to myself just as one of the men walked into the room holding two screaming beagles by the scruff of their necks.

"Let them go!" I demanded, no longer able to stay quiet. I started to get out of the chair when the girl pushed me back down.

"Sit!" she yelled as she fished through her pocket and pulled out a knife. "Tell us where our dogs are, or these ones are as good as dead."

Instinct kicked in and I threw as hard a punch as my hundred pound frame could manage. It wasn't enough to knock her off her feet, but it definitely threw her off guard as she staggered backward. It didn't take long to get her bearings back and this time she came toward me with the knife.

"My friend has the dogs!" I lied.

Not pleased with my answer she took another step toward me before Rob stopped her.

"Where are they?" he boomed, pushing the girl out of the way so he could stand directly over top of me.

"I don't know where he has them. He just said that they were safe." I lied again. "I can call him in the morning and tell him to bring them to my house." If they bought all these lies I was throwing out, I might have enough time for Trish to figure things out and send help.

"Call now!" than man urged, coming even closer.

"It's the middle of the night, he isn't going to answer," I replied, irritated. "It's only a few hours from morning. I'll call then."

"Fine, but don't get any bright ideas," the man began, "and give me your phone. You can have it back to call and that's it."

Reluctantly I handed over my phone and slouched back into the chair to wait for day break to come. The two beagles were still pacing nervously around the room, looking for a way out. I could definitely relate to them as I anxiously awaited my own fate. I wondered where they had come from as I didn't recognize them from the shelter. It didn't appear they had been used yet so they must be new. Unsure of where they had them hidden before bringing them out to be massacred, I thought of how many other dogs might be stashed away behind closed doors. It made me feel nauseous thinking about how many animals they hurt in the process of turning their pits into fighting machines.

Having been over 24 hours since I had slept, my eyes began to burn as I felt my body slowly begin shutting down.. I used to pull all nighters quite often back in California, maybe it was different when alcohol and mobs of people were involved. Sitting here alone in the room, with the exception of Jess, I had discovered the snarky woman's name to be, I began to doze in and out of consciousness.

At some point I must had fallen asleep, as I woke up to a chaos of noise suddenly erupting from the front of the house. Jumping to her feet, Jess ran toward the commotion, leaving me there alone with the girl who still lay passed out in the same position. Just as I got to my feet to make a run for it, everyone came charging down the hallway and past the room where I stood, dazed and confused.

Before I could make any decisions, I heard the front door get kicked in and several voices yelling. I couldn't make out what they were saying, but it didn't sound good. I debated whether or not I should hide and frantically looked around the room for a good spot. What if this was some gang fight. I definitely didn't want in the middle of that. Trish was right, I shouldn't have come back.

"Hands up in the air where I can see them!" yelled a voice behind me. I spun around and threw my arms up. Relief flooded through me when I saw the blue outfit the man had on with the Police insignia. Before the officer got to me, everything began to get fuzzy and I felt myself spinning. What was happening to me. The room got darker.

And darker.

Then nothing…I saw nothing.

I briefly came to, and felt myself being carried by someone. Trying to talk, I felt my chest tighten and the words get stuck. I couldn't make a sound. Then it went black again.

It felt like I was on a boat in the middle of the ocean, yet I could hear sirens and people talking all around me. I tried to open my eyes but couldn't seem to figure out how. All I could focus on was the shooting pain that kept running through my leg. It would only make it half way up and then go away. Over and over again, like something was preventing it from going all the way up my leg to my hip. Almost like it wasn't attached to the rest of my body.

"Karen!" I heard someone yell once the boat reached shore. I thought I recognized the voice but I couldn't put my finger on it. If only I could see them I might be able to figure it out, but I still wasn't able to open my eyes. Or talk.

Then it felt like I was floating. I wasn't swaying in the ocean anymore, it was different now. Like whatever I was on was just hovering in the air. I could tell I was moving, but didn't understand how. I knew I was laying down, I could feel the pressure on my back. Something had me stuck though and I couldn't turn my head. If only I could find a way to open my eyes maybe everything would make sense.

People kept calling my name. I didn't recognize any of these voices though, only the first one who had been there when I got off the boat. Someone kept poking my leg with something sharp and I wanted to tell them to stop, but still couldn't find my voice. It wasn't painful, just annoying. Why couldn't everyone just leave me alone.

It felt like an eternity had passed when I finally started to feel the grogginess lift. Voices were no longer muffled and I could clearly hear what people were saying for the first time.

"Is she going to be ok?" someone asked. They were standing next to my bed with their hand on my arm. I recognized that voice! It was Trish!

"She lost a lot of blood and is probably still in shock," a voice replied. "She should wake up soon though."

I heard footsteps grow fainter as I presume someone left the room, then a door clicked shut. The hand that had been resting on my arm was now moving something around on my face.

"These stupid tubes," I heard her say. I could feel a weird pressure in my nose as she moved what I gathered to be an oxygen tube around.

I felt my eyelids start to flutter.

"Karen? Can you hear me?" Trish asked softly.

I still couldn't find my voice, so I shook my head yes.

"Everything's going to be alright," she told me as she lightly ran her fingers through my hair. "You're going to be alright."

For some reason her reassuring words calmed me, and I felt my body go limp again.

I didn't know how much time had passed, but when I finally woke up Trish was still there next to my bed. Adjusting my eyes to the light, I squinted at the clock to see the time. "Annie!" I whispered, bolting up off my pillow. "Trish, we have to find Annie, she got loose last night when I got caught and is probably terrified out in those woods alone."

Trish laid a calming hand on my arm, "Annie will be fine. You need to lay back down, the doctor said you lost a lot of blood and need to stay in bed for a while."

"I can't stay here while she is out there alone, and all the dogs at the kennel, I have to get home to them!" Scrambling to get out of bed, I felt a pain course through my leg as I ripped off the covers.

Half my left leg was bandaged up so tight I was sure it was cutting of circulation. Last night's events came flooding back. "Did they catch them?"

"They caught the girl and one of the guys, but they said another ran off on foot and they didn't have enough back up to spare an officer to track him," Trish replied, helping me back into a comfortable position. "I've already been to the kennel, everyone is fed and I put new blankets down."

"What about all the dogs on the property? Did they say what would happen to them?" I asked, fearing the worse. Most of the dogs there would be too aggressive to put up for adoption if they ended up in a shelter. They would all be euthanized.

"I haven't heard much," Trish admitted. "One of the cops seemed to be taking charge of the situation. He said he knew you?"

"I don't know any cops around here," I confessed, baffled at why one would think he knew me.

"Well you'll find out today," Trish laughed, "he said he would be back this afternoon to check on you."

This left my head spinning. I didn't know anyone around here, let alone a cop. And I hadn't gotten into any trouble so how would one recognize me.

"He was really good looking too," Trish added, poking me in the side.

We talked awhile longer before the pain medication began to kick in, making me drowsy. I fought it for as long as possible, but eventually I gave in and sank back into the weird black abyss. Feeling myself float away, I heard Trish's voice get softer and softer and then nothing at all. Once again, I was in this other world dimension where nothing existed.

CHAPTER 4

This time when I woke up, Trish was gone and I was all alone. A sudden fear overtook me and I quickly pushed the assistance button next to my bed. When no one came right away, I pushed it several more times. Finally the nurse I had recognized from earlier strolled through the door and asked if everything was alright.

"Where is Trish?" I demanded, surprised at the panic I could hear in my own voice.

"She said she would be back tonight," the nurse reassured me. "Told me to tell you that everything was taken care of and that you shouldn't worry about a thing."

Figuring she had gone to take care of the dogs, I relaxed slightly and leaned back against the pillow. "Ok," I replied, a little more calmly this time.

"You have another visitor however," the nurse began, "he told me to get him when you woke up. Are you feeling well enough to have visitors?"

"Yea I feel fine," I lied. Truth was, my head was pounding and I felt like I was just waking up from a whole weekend of nonstop drinking. "You can send him in."

The nurse left to fetch who I guessed was the police officer that Trish had told me about. Still baffled at who it could be, I patiently waited, fighting to stay awake the whole time. Whatever they had pumping though the IV was some good stuff.

Just as I was about to pass back out, I heard a knock on the door. Eyes half glazed over, I lifted my head to see who this mystery guest was and gasped when I recognized the man standing in the door way.

Even in his police uniform I immediately recognized him, I mean with a face like his it was hard to forget. "Eric?"

"How are you feeling? Are they taking good care of you here?" he asked as he walked into the room, letting the door close behind him.

"I'm feeling alright," I replied, trying to push the grogginess aside. Terrified of what I must look like, I quickly ran my fingers through what I guessed looked like a matted mess of hair. "You're a cop?"

"Does that surprise you?" he laughed.

"Well, kind of I guess," I replied, feeling stupid. Obviously he was a cop or why else would he be wearing a cops uniform?

"I was the one of the officers that was assigned to the call," he smiled. "Your friend, Trish, contacted us yesterday morning saying she thought something bad had happened and that her friend might be in danger. You can only imagine how surprised I was to find you there."

"How much trouble am I going to be in?" I asked, knowing full well there were going to be consequences for trespassing and theft.

"I can't answer that," he sighed. "I don't know where the case will go. No one is in any position to press charges at this time."

"What is going to happen to all the dogs?" I dreaded the answer to this question. For some reason, finding out how much trouble I might be in was easier to swallow then finding out what would happen with all those dogs. I wasn't sure if anyone was aware that I had a warehouse full of their dogs, but I wasn't going to bring it up until they did.

"Well, I can't really answer that either," he apologized. "Right now I know they are being held at a shelter in Atlanta until further notice."

Feeling tears begin welling up in my eyes, I turned my head away so he wouldn't see them spill over. I knew exactly how this would end for those dogs. He must have seen the pain I was in because before I could say anything he put his hand on my arm and told me he was doing everything he could.

Just as I was about to thank him, the door creaked open and Trish walked in.

"Sorry, should I come back?" she quickly asked, seeing Eric standing next to the bed.

"No, you can come in," I smiled, wiping the tears from my face. I was about to introduce them to each other, when I remembered they had already met.

"I should get going anyway," Eric began, "I just wanted to stop in and see how you were doing." Genuine concern filled those piercing blue eyes, as he squeezed my arm and told me to get better soon.

Once he had left the room, Trish gave me the biggest I told you so smile. "Okay, spill!" She laughed. "How do you know him! And where the heck did he come from! He must be Latino or something."

"He came in to the shelter the other day, looking to adopt another pit. We didn't have any that were young enough, so I told him about Reina. Well, not everything about her, just that she was a young pit and I was fostering her." For the first time all day, I wasn't feeling loopy from the meds, I didn't know what I was feeling. Embarrassed was definitely on top of the list, however. I couldn't even imagine what I looked like, and here this drop dead gorgeous man was making time out of his day to check in on me.

"Well, I can tell you this much," Trish giggled, "he is definitely into you." She pulled up a chair next to the bed and sat down beside me. "Don't tell me you're not interested, because if that's the case..."

Before she could finish I cut in. "Well of course I'm interested! A girl would have to be blind not to be! Look at me though! I can't believe I let him see me looking like this."

Trish bust out laughing. "You do look like a bit of a homeless person."

I lightly punched her in the arm jokingly. He would disappear for good after seeing me today, not that I had looked much better the other day when we first met.

Trish's facial expression went from fun to serious all of a sudden, as something must have popped into her head. "So, I called your parents," she said hesitantly, looking down at her hands.

"You what?" I exclaimed. A feeling of panic began to well up inside me. "Why would you do that Trish!"

"One of the officers said that you might be looking at some serious fines," she replied. "I explained everything to your parents. I knew you couldn't afford them on your own and I was hoping they might help."

"They're not going to help," I explained, telling her how I hadn't heard from them in months. They didn't care.

"Well, I don't think that's the case," she whispered, still not making eye contact.

"What's going on?" I knew that look on her face, she rarely got nervous, especially not around me.

"They'll be here tonight," she finally replied. "I didn't mean to get you in trouble, I was just trying to help.

I wasn't mad at Trish, she did what she thought was right. Maybe they wouldn't be as mad as I was imagining. "It's alright, they would have found out eventually," I reassured her.

"I went out to your house today and looked for Annie," she changed the subject. "Looked all over the woods and drove up and down the nearby roads. I even stopped and asked a few of the neighbors if they had seen any loose dogs lately, unfortunately no one had. Maybe the precinct that took all the dogs off the property found her."

"She probably stayed close by, which would make since. As soon as I get out of here I want to go to Atlanta and find out if they have her with the rest of the seized dogs."

"I'll go with you," Trish offered. "Maybe if you take her paperwork from the shelter they will work with you."

"We can stop by and grab it on the way," I began, "Elaine might know what to do. We can fill her in and see what she suggests."

The rest of the day was spent dreading my parents arrival. It wasn't my dad I was worried about, my mom on the other hand, she scared me. For being a small woman like myself, she could make just about anyone cower. It must have been the Italian in her.

While I sat there alone and waited, I decided to send Eric a quick text, thanking him for stopping by earlier. After an hour passed and I still didn't get a response, I figured I must had scared him off with my homeless appearance.

The nurse entered the room just as I was checking my phone for what I told myself was the last time. I wasn't sure if I was glad they had found and returned it or not. Waiting for him to text back was making my heart race.

"You feel like having a visitor?" she asked while checking the monitor I was still hooked up to.

I hesitated before nodded my head, figuring I might as well get it over with. Here we go, I thought to myself.

As the door opened, I wanted to crawl under the blankets and disappear. Instead I put on the bravest face I could muster and stared down at my hands.

"Hey," a gentle voice whispered, definitely not my parents.

My head jerked up as I recognized the voice. "Hey!" I replied trying not to sound as excited as I felt. Seeing a bouquet of flowers in his hand, I tried to push back the goofy smile that I felt creep across my face.

"I just wanted to bring these by." He sat the flowers on the table next to my bed. "You seemed pretty upset earlier and I wanted to cheer you up."

Cheer me up was an understatement, I was on cloud nine. "Well, thank you," I replied at a loss for words. "You didn't have to do that."

"I know, but I wanted to," he smiled. "You seem to be having a rough day."

"Rough year would be more like it," I laughed.

"What were you doing at that place anyway? We're you really trying to steal their dogs?" he asked, more intrigued than anything.

He must not have known about the warehouse, I thought, bringing a sense of relief. The last thing I wanted was to have all those dogs confiscated and put in a shelter where I knew they would end up euthanized for aggression, especially Jaxx.

"Well, yea, that was the plan," I replied nervously. "I live right next door and had been watching them for a while. I knew they were up to no good over there."

"Why didn't you come to the police?" he asked.

"I was told there had to be evidence of dog fighting in order for them to do anything about it. I didn't think a bunch of dogs chained up outside would be enough to make a case," I answered, realizing I probably should have listened to Trish and let the police handle it.

"I understand," he replied sadly. "I just wish it hadn't come to this. The two men that were arrested were being tracked by the animal cruelty office out of Atlanta. They must had been staying low and hiding out the past few months as the case got pushed to the back. There are more dog fighting operations than you can imagine out here."

"I had no idea," I apologized. "I just wanted to get the dogs out of there and was afraid if I took it to the police and nothing got done they would disappear.

We were mid conversation when the door flew open and my mom burst inside. Seeing the look of fear in my eyes, Eric quickly jumped up and extended a hand. "I'm officer O'Dell."

Ignoring the fact that he was trying to shake her hand, mom looked at me and then back at Eric. "Why are you talking to my daughter without a lawyer present?" she demanded.

"Oh," Eric began, probably feeling the same fear everyone felt when my mom spoke. "It's not like that ma'am."

"He's a friend of mine," I quickly added.

"Well then he will understand that he needs to leave so we can talk to you in private," my mom replied, pointing to the door.

"Mother!" I growled, surprised at being able to confront her, "you're being rude!"

Eric flashed me a quick smile and snuck out the room before I could apologize.

"I understand you're upset with me," I told my mom. "You don't have to take it out on my friends though."

"We're not upset honey," my dad chimed in for the first time. "We're worried about you, maybe it's time you come home for a while."

"I'm not going anywhere," I demanded. "I have a life here now, one that I actually like."

I'm pretty sure this surprised my parents as much as it did me. A year ago I would have jumped at the chance to move back to California. Not now though, I had way to much going on here to just up and leave. I wondered how much Trish had told my parents, if they knew about the dogs I had rescued or that I was living in a warehouse and working at a shelter.

"We talked to Trish," my dad began, "she was adamant we come out to see what you were up to and how much you've changed."

This earned me an eye roll from my mom.

"It doesn't seem like she changed to me," my mom added. "Seems like the same old Karen, never thinking of the consequences for her actions."

"Maybe we should let her explain, Julia," my dad sternly replied.

A lot had obviously changed since I moved out. Never in my life had I seen my dad stand up to my mom.

"What is there to explain Robert, she broke the law and might end up in jail." Looking at me she added, "this is coming out of your inheritance money."

"No one is even sure what kind of punishment I'm looking at," I retorted angrily. "Eric said they might not even push for charges."

"Oh, Eric said," my mom sneered. "Well we talked to our lawyer this morning and the amount it's going to take for this all to be swept under the rug is not small."

"What do you mean you talked to a lawyer this morning?" I asked. "You don't even know the whole situation, how could someone give you a price on something I'm not convicted of yet."

"You're not going to be convicted of anything, this whole ordeal is going to stay quiet. I will not have you dirty the family name," she replied, looking at my dad for back up.

I was surprised when it didn't come. Instead, my dad insisted that we hear both sides of the story before jumping to any conclusions. So, reluctantly I told them about everything that had happened the past two years, hoping it wouldn't come back to bite me.

Neither of my parents said a word when I finished talking, they both just stood there staring at me. I couldn't tell if they were mad or disappointed, or what they were feeling.

Finally, after what seemed to be forever, my dad smiled and told me he was proud of me. Looking at his wife he waited for her response, or maybe a fist to the face for condoning 'bad behavior'."

"You're telling me that you lost your good job, have been working for minimum wage while living in a warehouse, and that you would rather stay here than go back home?" she stammered.

"I need to stay here for the dogs," I pointed out, not surprised she only heard what she wanted. "They have nowhere to go if I leave."

"Well I think that is a very mature thing to do," my father praised. "I'm happy for you honey, and I'm glad you've finally grown up and moved out of the party scene. I honestly never thought it would happen."

"I'm glad you're not partying anymore as well," my mother piped in. "I don't agree with what you did however. You should have let the authorities take care of it and stayed out of trouble."

This was as good as a compliment coming from her. She was never the loving mother type, running a multimillion-dollar business and having everyone fear her was her thing. Coddling a child, on the other hand, was not.

"What happens now?" I asked, regarding what she said about the lawyer. "Will I have to go to court?"

"I told you, it's all been taken care of. At your expense, I might add," my mom replied as she left the room.

Feeling like I could finally take a breath after she was gone, I looked at my dad and smiled. We had always had a close relationship, it was him that I went to anytime I needed a parent. "You're not mad at me?"

"Absolutely not," he replied giving me a hug. "I couldn't be more proud. What you're doing is exactly what your grandmother would have wanted. You've found what makes you happy, and worked for it. That's all we wanted. Getting yourself in trouble, wasn't exactly in the plan, but it shows your willing to fight for what you believe in."

I knew this wouldn't be enough to get my inheritance, and I didn't even care. The money would be nice, but that wasn't what I was about anymore.

Sensing what was going through my head, my dad smiled. "Your gram told me that I could give you a portion of your inheritance when I saw fit, and I think you could use it right now. When I get back home I will transfer some money into your account."

I couldn't believe what he was saying. "Thank you, dad," I whispered as tears filled my eyes. They had no way of knowing how much this would help.

"It won't be much," he warned, trying not to get my hopes up. "With the lawyer fees and all that, your mom probably won't let me send much. I'll see what I can do though."

We said our goodbyes as dad made it clear mom didn't want to be here long. I wished I could spend time out of the hospital with just my dad, and show him everything I was doing. He wasn't exactly an animal lover, but he did appreciate effort, and that was something I was giving a lot of these days

As soon as everyone was gone, and I had the room to myself again, I checked my phone to see if Trish had text. Shocked at all the unread messages that popped up, I clicked into the message folder to see who they were from. Three from Trish, of course she would be worried about how things went with my parents and would want to hear all about it, and one from Eric.

Without hesitation, I opened Eric's text first, curious as to what he had to say after my mom so rudely kicked him out.

"Karen, I'm sorry if I caused any trouble with your parents. I hope things calmed down after I left. I wanted to talk to you about something, but maybe I will get that chance another day. I hope you like your flowers and can get out of that place soon.

Wow, I thought to myself, he really does seem like a good guy. That was rare with how attractive he was, usually guys that looked like him were full of themselves and couldn't care less about what someone else was going through.

The messages from Trish were exactly what I expected.

"Hey"

"What's going on, why aren't you texting me back?"

"Karen, is everything okay!? Text me back now, I'm freaking out! Are your parents still there? Do you want me to come up?"

Exactly what I had expected. I quickly messaged her back letting her know everything was fine and that I had some good news to tell her.

Just as I was about to reply to Eric's message, the nurse walked in and told me that the doctor said it was ok for me to go home in the morning. This might had been the best news I heard all day, but my dad beat them to it.

Before texting Eric, I shot Trish a message telling her I could be picked up bright and early tomorrow morning, and that I would be forever grateful if she got me the heck out of this place.

I'm so sorry for the way my mom treated you, she is like that with everyone so I hope you didn't take too much offense. Things got a lot better after she left and it was just me and my dad, he actually gave me some really good news. And to top it all off the nurse just came in and told me I could go home in the morning.

As soon as I pushed send, I remembered he had told me there was something he wanted to talk to me about, so I send another message.

What is it you wanted to talk to me about?

It was after 8'oclock and I was beginning to get tired, so I set the phone on the pillow, hoping it would wake me up if either of them replied.

Clearly, I was much more tired that I had though. It wasn't until morning when I woke up to Trish shaking my arm. Curious of the time, I peeked at my phone and saw a missed call and several messages.

"Its six in morning," I laughed sleepily, "you didn't have to come this early."

"Well I figured you would be anxious to see the dogs," she replied, "and I couldn't sleep after you told me you had some good news to tell me."

I had almost forgot! "My dad is going to transfer some of my inheritance into my account!" I screeched. Excitement took over as I bounded out of bed, and headed for the door. "Let's go!"

I didn't know if the money had hit my account yet, but I was too excited to wait any longer to find out. After checking myself out at the front desk, we searched the parking lot for Trish's car.

"You always do this," I laughed. "I don't understand how someone can forget where they parked every time they leave their car."

Finally, after searching the entire parking lot, we found her car and headed for the warehouse. By the time we had all the dogs fed and morning chores finished, the bank would be open.

After being stuck in the stuffy hospital room for the past 2 days, it felt good being outside in the fresh air. I couldn't wait to start getting the dogs out for their walks and enjoy the sunshine.

"So, I see you got flowers," Trish pointed at the bouquet I had gently placed on the back seat. "I'm guessing those weren't from your parents."

"No, definitely not," I laughed. Sometimes it surprised me at how well we knew each other, but I guess that came with being best friends ever since we were kids. "Eric brought them up yesterday right before my parents got there. Then my mom scared him away, or should I say chased."

"You met the guy once, and he shows up at the hospital to check on you and brings you flowers." Turning into the warehouse parking lot, she looked at me with a huge smile on her face. "Now do you believe me that he's interested in you?"

That reminded me, I hadn't check my phone since she picked me up and I had messages. Frantically I searched my pockets, and was relieved to find I hadn't left it at the hospital in my rush to get out of there.

"I have a message from him!" I squealed, feeling like a high school girl again.

"Well what's it say!" She asked, equally as excited.

No worries, I've dealt with a lot worse. Lol. I can't wait to hear this good news that has you so excited!

He hadn't mentioned what it was that he wanted to talk to me about, so I resent the text. Maybe he didn't get it.

We barely got in the kennel when my phone went off, alerting me I had a text. Since I was with Trish and no one else ever text me, I knew it was Eric and eagerly fished the phone from my pocket.

I was hoping maybe we could talk over dinner one night this week.

It was hard to make time for anything other than work and the dogs, but I wasn't about to turn him down. Showing Trish the message, she confirmed my thoughts.

"You have to go!" she exclaimed, face glowing with excitement.

"I want to, but how am I going to make time with everything else that is going on?" I replied, trying not to let myself get to excited.

"Well, you could always tell him about this place." She grabbed a few of the food bowls and began filling them. "He seems to really love dogs."

"He is a cop though," I reminded her. "What if he says something or tells me I have to turn the dogs I got off the property over to them?"

Seeing how restless the dogs were becoming, we began to pass out the food before they climbed out of their kennels to get it themselves. I didn't actually think they could until I looked over at Jaxx, who had made it halfway up and was peeking over at me.

"Jaxx! Get down!" I gently demanded as I slid his breakfast in to him. I would have to fix that so he couldn't climb over.

The rest of the dogs bounced from wall to wall, eagerly waiting for us to make our rounds. As soon as everyone was eating and the kennel was quiet, Trish made her way over and helped me gather all the water buckets to clean.

"I really don't think he would tell anyone," she began as she dropped the last few buckets into the huge standing sink. "He really seems to like you, and cop or not, he is still a guy."

"I don't know if I can risk it," I replied. My trust in people wasn't all that great, and this was one thing I couldn't put into the hands of someone I didn't know very well.

"What if you didn't tell him that some of the dogs here were stolen, and that they were just strays or dogs from your shelter," she advised.

I still wasn't sure that was something I was willing to do, not only would I already be lying to him, but who knows what the guys told the cops. It was possible that was what he had wanted to talk to me about.

"I don't know, maybe down the road I will, but I don't think it's a good idea just yet," I admitted. "I'll text him back and say I can meet later in the evening, that way all the chores will be done. I can get the dogs out for a longer walk after dinner instead of doing it while we clean."

"Or, you could go to dinner and enjoy yourself and I can do the chores," Trish suggested, handing me the last of the freshly cleaned buckets. "After all, you did just take a bullet to the leg a few days ago, you deserve a break."

"No way. I can't let you do all the work while I'm out enjoying myself," I answered as we began filling the buckets with water. "I'll find a way to make it work, besides, my leg feels better when I keep it moving. "

"I really don't mind," she insisted, "it isn't like I have anything else to do anyway."

Trish and I were the complete opposite in high school. She had always stuck to herself and really didn't have any other friends other than myself. Not much had changed in college. She rarely hung out with anyone from school or work, other than her roommate, Ashley.

"If he can't meet up after chores, I might take you up on your offer," I laughed, knowing she wouldn't take no for an answer. Pulling out my phone, I shot Eric a text saying I could meet up any time after eight.

As soon as the kennels were cleaned, we headed up town to go to the bank. I didn't know what to expect when I asked for my balance, I only hoped it would be enough to get the warehouse cleaned up and maybe some more kennels. My weekly checks were enough to cover rent and the loan for the warehouse, and with giving up the house soon, I would have more than enough to survive. However, I needed to find a way to rescue the rest of the dogs that were seized off the neighbor's property. I couldn't let them get euthanized just because they were deemed aggressive. There had to be a way to rehabilitate them. Reina was already able to be walked with both of my dogs, and was growing more and more comfortable each day. There had to be hope for the others.

The lady behind the desk was taking her time as she navigated her way around the computer. She had to be a new worker, it never took this long any other time. Finally she printed off the balance and handed it over.

My jaw hit the floor.

"How much did he deposit?" Trish gasped, seeing the expression on my face.

I handed her the statement and smiled. I was expecting a few grand, maybe ten or twenty. I don't know how my dad convinced my mom to send this much, but the statement showed fifty thousand dollars was in my account.

"Oh my gosh!" Trish cheered, jumping up and down. "You can turn that place into a whole new building with that much money!"

"I know!" I exclaimed. "Where do we even start!"

Our outburst of excitement had everyone in the lobby staring, probably wondering what was going on. I felt like I had just hit the jack pot!

Feeling it was safer to leave the money in my account and just write checks, we sat in the car as I made a few phone calls. First things first, we would need a giant dumpster so we could clear the building out. I wished I had a network of friends here to help, the more money we could save by doing everything our self, meant more to use on rescuing dogs.

"Text Ashley and see if she and her boyfriend would want to help," I told Trish. I didn't know her roommate very well, but the few times we had met she seemed really nice. Since she was also going to vet school, I was sure she wouldn't mind helping a rescue out. Not that I was an actual licensed rescue yet, but the process was in the works.

"You could ask Eric if he wants to help," Trish prodded. "I'm pretty sure he would say yes!"

"Maybe I will," I laughed at her determination to get us together.

After all the texts had been sent and a dumpster scheduled to be delivered that afternoon, we made our way to the shelter I worked at to gather Annie's paperwork before making the trip to Atlanta.

Thankfully, my incident fell on my weekend off so I only had to miss one day of work while in the hospital. Elaine was more than understanding when I called yesterday and told her I wouldn't be in and that I needed a personal day. I didn't tell her what for, so when I explained it in person after asking to speak in private, she just stood there in shock.

"Are you in trouble?" she finally asked, concerned.

"I don't think so, my parents spoke with a lawyer and it's all being taken care of," I replied.

"Where do they had the dogs on hold at? I will call them right now and fax over Annie's paperwork," she asked, taking charge of the situation.

I was glad to have Elaine on my side, she was a force to be reckoned with when it came to the welfare of dogs. I knew she would get everything taken care of, so after giving her the information, Trish and I headed back home to get started on our latest project. It was hard leaving Annie's fate in the hands of someone else, but I knew Elaine would do everything in her power to get Annie back.

Walking into the warehouse I found myself not knowing where to start. We had already moved most of the clutter to one side of the main room, but hadn't touched the others yet. Each room was packed full, some with furniture that was too big for the two of us to move. I was relieved when Trish's phone went off with a message from Ashely saying they would be over soon. It was still early so I didn't expect to hear anything from Eric for a while.

Thankfully, the dumpster was delivered just as Ashely pulled into the parking lot. The less time we spent standing around staring at everything, the more we could get done.

Before we got started, Ashely asked if she could have a quick tour of the kennel to meet all the dogs. Just as we were heading in, my phone went off so I sent Trish in to show them around while I read the message.

Evenings work great for me, I get off work at five. If that's too early we can meet up whenever works best for you. I look forward to seeing you soon.

I wondered if today would be too soon, as I sent him a message asking if he wanted to come over after his shift and help me with a project. I was hesitant to send it, seeing how everything could go up in smoke if he ratted me out. There was no turning back now though, the message showed delivered next to it.

Text me the address and I will be there around six. What kind of project am I getting myself into? Hopefully one that won't end up with us in jail or the hospital, lol.

Walking into the kennel still laughing at his message, I found Trish in front of Diamonds kennel, explaining how she was scheduled to be euthanized the day I rescued her. Ashely turned around when she heard me walk up and began thanking me for helping all the dogs in here. She pointed to the kennel with Jaxx inside and said that he was her favorite. That was shocking, as all he was doing was bouncing from one side to the other, barking his head off.

"He needs a lot of work," I pointed out. "He has the worst case of dog aggression I have ever seen, but is a total sweetheart when it comes to people."

I was glad to see Trish had given both the visitors treats to hand out. It was important for the dogs to associate new people with something positive. It helped to teach them to stay calm when someone approached their kennel. I wished we had the chance to do this with all the dogs at the shelter, as most of them were so barrier aggressive it was hard to get them adopted. No one wanted a dog that lunged at the gate growling and barking.

As we made our way to the room we planned on cleaning out first, I pulled Trish aside and excitedly told her that Eric would be here in a few hours.

"Oh my gosh are you serious? He is really going to come help?" she chirped. "He is absolutely, without a doubt into you!"

"I think he might be!" I giggled.

We set to work sorting through everything, putting the junk in the dumpster, and anything that was still in decent shape aside. With four of us working, it didn't take long before I noticed progress. Unlike the other night where it took all evening just to make a dent in the room.

I received a text from Eric telling me he was a few minutes away, so I left the three to continue cleaning as I went out to the parking lot to meet him. As I walked past Trish, she smiled and nudged me.

"You go girl," she laughed.

He must had gotten lost, as ten minutes passed before a black suburban pulled in. I had never thought about what he might drive, but for some reason I had him pegged for a sports car kind of guy. SUVs struck me as more of a family vehicle, not something a single hot guy would be driving.

I was shocked when he got out and gave me a hug, and more flowers.

"I hope I didn't keep you waiting. I wasn't expecting the address you gave me to lead to a warehouse," he laughed.

Thanking him for the flowers, I gave him a quick run down of what we were doing here. Of course, I left out where the money came from and the fact that some of the dogs inside were stolen.

"Wow, so you work at a shelter all day, then come home afterward and run a rescue. I'm impressed." He followed me into the building after I told him I would show him around.

"So most of these dogs were going to be put to sleep at the shelter and you took them home instead?" he asked once we finished the tour.

"That's right," I lied. I felt bad not telling him the truth, but I still wasn't comfortable laying it all on the line yet.

"You're like their angel," he smiled.

Blushing at his compliment, I led the way to where everyone was hard at work. "I guess you could say that," I smiled back, "but I like to think of them as my angels instead."

Thinking about where I was at in my life a year ago, it brought me immeasurable joy to be free from the bitterness and rage I had harbored inside for so long. Being kicked out of my home and having to move away from my friends caused me so much anger when I had first moved here, but that all changed after I started rescuing dogs.

After a quick introduction, everyone set to work clearing out the remainder of the furniture. I felt bad that everyone was working so hard to help me, and I didn't even have anything to offer them to eat and drink. Pulling Trish aside, I handed her some money and asked if she would run up the road and grab a few pizzas and soda.

The two guys did most of the heavy lifting, leaving Ashley and I to work together while Trish was gone. Since most of the clutter was finally moved out, we set to work sweeping up all the dirt and debris. The room already looked way better and I couldn't wait to get faux grass floor laid. I had always seen pictures of these luxury boarding facilities in Atlanta, and I wanted to make the warehouse as comfortable as I could for the rescue residents. Most of the dogs in my care never knew love or had a good home, and it was my goal to give them everything they never had.

We took a break and ate dinner together as soon as Trish returned with the food. I didn't normally eat a lot and was surprised when I found myself demolishing half a pizza by myself.

"Where do you put all that food?" Ashely joked. "I have to know your secret to staying so skinny!"

Trish and I both laughed, knowing how my normal meals wouldn't fill up a bird. Ever since I was little, I had a problem with my self image and was terrified of gaining weight. I took a lot of pride in my perfect figure and worked hard to keep it that way. Since moving to Georgia, I found myself caring a lot more about things that actually mattered, than I did about my image. I was pretty sure I went up a size or two in the past year.

Just as it was turning dark and everyone was getting ready to leave, Eric asked if we could take one of the dogs out together for a walk. I was more than happy to comply with his request, especially since Trish wasn't there to help me with Jaxx. The rest of the dogs I could walk on my own.

I explained how he had to be walked as I hooked both leashes to his collar and handed him one. There could be no chance in him escaping with how aggressive he was toward other animals. The last thing the breed needed was more negative media, which is exactly what I feared would happen if he got loose.

"How come he is so aggressive toward other dogs?" Eric asked once we had him outside and calmed down. "He is so friendly with people."

I didn't know how to answer that without blowing my cover, so I simply shrugged and told him that some dogs just don't get along with others. I had seen plenty come into the shelter with some degree of dog aggression, and they weren't fighting dogs. I didn't have much experience with training, so I just dealt with his issues the only way I knew how and that was by protecting him from a situation that he would fail at. Now that I had extra money, I could afford to hire someone to help me train him and the others so they were more adoptable.

It was the warmest night we had in a while, so I was in no hurry to end the walk. The company certainly wasn't bad either. Making conversation with Eric was easy, as all we talked about was dogs. He told me about his pit bull, and how he had rescued him from a shelter in Atlanta a year ago.

"I wasn't raised around the breed, so I believed everything I heard about how dangerous they were," he confessed. "It wasn't until I got Axel that I seen first hand how wrong I was."

"That's how I was!" I agreed, understanding exactly where he was coming from. "A dog named Rey changed my whole outlook on pit bulls, now they're by far my favorite breed."

"Is that why most of the dogs you have are pits?" he asked curiously.

"Well, that and the fact that they are the usually the first on the list to get euthanized. Everyone is either too afraid to adopt them, or cant because they rent, and you know how that goes. I just wish there was a way to change people's minds and make them see what great dogs they are."

"I agree," he smiled. "Your enthusiasm for rescuing is really remarkable. Most girls your age, especially the pretty ones, are too absorbed in themselves to care about this sort of stuff. I really like how dedicated you are."

I didn't know what to say. The hottest guy on the planet just called me pretty, that alone sent a swirl of butterflies through my stomach. He had a crazy way of making me feel like everything I was working so hard for, was actually being noticed. I couldn't get over how different he was from the men back home.

"Thank you," I smiled, feeling my cheeks turn warm. Thankfully it was dark out and he couldn't see how red I was sure they had turned.

"So tell me," he began, "are any of the dogs inside part of the bust we made the other day?"

My heart sank and all the butterflies seemed to go away as quickly as they had come. I couldn't find any words to say, so I quickly looked down so my facial expression wouldn't give me away.

"I'm not going to tell anyone if they are," he added before I could figure out what to say. "I know I could get in trouble for keeping it a secret, but I don't want to see any more dogs caged up on hold for court. Especially with their past, dogs like that rarely make it out alive."

"You really wont report it?" I asked, astonished. "Couldn't you lose your job!"

"Yea, I could. That's only if they found out I knew though," he replied. "So if you don't tell my secret, I won't tell yours.

"You really are amazing," I blurted out before I could stop myself. "I mean.."

"Wait, could you just repeat that?" Even in the dark I could see his blue eyes sparkle, matching his perfect smile. "Did you just call me amazing?"

"Yea, I guess I did." I laughed hesitantly. I was sure he heard that all the time.

"Well, my night has been made," he laughed back.

We were just getting back to the warehouse and had to cut our conversation short in order to focus on getting Jaxx safely back in his kennel. It was never an easy task getting him past all the other dogs, as he tried dragging us toward them.

"I've never seen a dog that powerful before," he gasped, just as out of breath as I was. "Is he one of them?"

Knowing exactly what he meant, I nodded my head. "When they caught me they said one of their dogs was worth more than my life. I'm guessing they were referring to him."

"No wonder he is so aggressive, they must have used him in a lot of fights if he is worth that much," he replied sadly.

"I'm just glad I was able to get him out of there before everything went down. Can you imagine him in some busy shelter? He would lose his mind."

"No kidding," he agreed. "I wish I didn't have to head out so early, but I'm on first shift tomorrow and it's a bit of a drive to get to my place from here."

"Thank you for helping me with Jaxx," I smiled as we walked toward his suburban. "Poor guy would have been stuck in there all night if you hadn't stayed and helped,"

"Anytime! I look forward to seeing you again soon," he said while giving me a quick hug goodnight.

I watched as he pulled out of the parking lot and drove off, then headed inside for the night. It was already too late to get anymore dogs out, so I grabbed my girls and made my way to the now clean room and hunkered down for the night.

Just as I was getting ready to lay down, my phone rang. Seeing Elaine's name pop up, I excitedly answered the call.

"What did you find out?" I asked, skipping the whole hello thing most people began a phone call with.

"I gave them her description," she began, "and they said they had two female pits that fit it. I went down after we closed for the day, and she was there. A little shaken up, but the vet that did her examination at their shelter said nothing was wrong with her. I was able to bring her back, but she has to remain on hold until the case is closed."

I breathed a sigh of relief and just sat there for a second trying to gather my thoughts before replying. "What about the other dogs? Did they say what would happen to them after the case was closed?"

"I only went for Annie, I didn't see the rest of them as they had her and the other female pit in a separate area waiting for me to arrive to verify if one of them was ours. I know this isn't what you want to hear, but the outcome for most cases like this isn't good. You have to stay focused on what you can do, and let go of what you cant."

She was right, that wasn't at all what I wanted to hear. I was beyond relieved that Annie was back in our care, but that didn't mean I didn't want to help the rest of the dogs that were seized from the property. They all deserved to have someone fight for them.

CHAPTER 5

The week flew by quickly, between working at the shelter and beginning the remodel of the warehouse, I didn't have time to do anything else. By the time the weekend rolled around, I felt like a lot had been accomplished. All of the lumber and flooring was due to arrive by this afternoon and everyone was planning on meeting at one o'clock to help move the kennels around and build the new rooms. Instead of keeping all the dogs in 10x10 chain link runs, I decided to put up private suites for them to make it less stressful. The room at the back of the building would serve as a holding area once the kennels were moved into there, that way new dogs could stay in there until they were vet checked and cleared of any contagious diseases.

I was just putting Reina back from her walk when I heard Eric pull in. He had kindly offered to help me move out of my old house since all I had was my car. I had already brought most of the small things over and just needed help moving the larger items, not that I had much.

Over the past week we had talked non-stop, and yesterday he came over to help me get some of the dogs out. He was quickly becoming someone I could rely on and trust.

"You ready to hit the road?" he asked, rolling down the window of the suburban.

Quickly locking the warehouse up, I ran over to the passenger side and got in. Sitting in the cup holder were two large coffee's.

"Half coffee, half sugar," he laughed, pointing to the one he got me. "Just how you like it."

"You're a life saver," I smiled, taking a sip of the delicious hot beverage. "I'm dragging this morning."

"You need to take a break one of these days. No one can go as hard as you do and not crash," he warned. "Let me take you out to dinner tomorrow."

"That's nice of you to offer, but I don't even know how I'm going to find the time to get everything done tomorrow, let alone find time to eat," I sighed. "Trish has to work late so she won't be able to help with evening chores so it's going to take me twice as long to get everything done."

"So I'll come by and help," he began as he merged onto the busy highway. "Then we can both have a relaxing evening once everything is done."

The highway was the quickest way to my old house, but I avoided it at all cost and stuck to the back roads. It was always busy with drivers who didn't pay attention, and after almost being run off the road twice, I swore I would never drive it again. Eric was a much better driver than I, however, and skillfully wove his way in and out of traffic.

"I guess that would work," I happily confessed. "I don't want to take up all your time though."

"I have nothing I would rather be doing." He looked at me and smiled as the breeze from the window carried the scent of his cologne toward me.

Inhaling deeply, I closed my eyes and savored the smell. There was no way this was happening, it was all too good to be true. There had to be a catch, or a down fall. Something had to be wrong with him, no one was this perfect.

Just as we were pulling into my driveway, his phone rang. "I've got to get this," he grumbled, "I'll just be a second."

While he was busy talking, I made my way inside to take one last look around to make sure I hadn't forgotten anything. Besides the couch, bed, and tv stand, the house was completely empty. It was a bittersweet feeling. Even though I hadn't spent much time here the past few months, it was still my first place I had on my own and a milestone in my life.

"Sorry about that," Eric mumbled as he joined me inside. "My job doesn't really understand days off."

"It's alright," I smiled. "You grab one end and I'll grab the other?" I pointed toward the couch, hoping I was strong enough to be of any help. Watching him lift his side effortlessly, I noticed his muscles tighten under the sleeves of his shirt.

"Are you going to grab your end?" he laughed, noticing I hadn't moved.

"Uh, yea. Sorry," I stammered, hoping it wasn't obvious that I was staring at him. The couch was a lot heavier than I remembered, as I strained every muscle in my body to lift it off the floor.

Waddling to keep up with him, we finally got the couch in the trailer without any accidents on my behalf. I thought for sure I was going to drop it several times and had to sink my fingers in so hard my hands were left throbbing. The rest of the furniture was easy to move, and before long we had everything strapped down and were on our way.

"Are you glad to be out of there?" he asked as we pulled out of the driveway. "It didn't seem like you stayed there very often."

"It's just easier to stay right at the kennel," I pointed out. "Saves a lot of time not having to drive back and forth.

"Makes sense," he laughed.

We had just finished unloading the trailer when everyone arrived. Thankfully, Ashely brought her boyfriend again and he ran up to help carry the couch the rest of the way into the building. My arms were growing tired and I didn't know how much longer I had before they gave out altogether.

As soon as they returned, I explained the game plan for the day and we got to work. Us girls took the dogs out while the two guys moved the kennels into the other room. Once all the dogs were moved out, we began building the suites.

The first two were up within an hour, so Trish and I started laying the tile floor while everyone else worked on constructing the next one. I couldn't wait for them to be finished and see the dog's reaction to their new homes.

"We have to get headed home," Ashley apologized. "We have dinner plans with Tom's parents and have already bailed once."

"Thanks for coming and helping out today," I replied, as we all walked outside together. "There's no way we would have gotten this much done without you."

"No problem," she smiled, "we will be over to help again soon."

There were only two suites left that needed to have the flooring done, so that's where Trish and I spent the remainder of the evening while Eric finished building the last room. For a bunch of novices, the place was looking pretty good.

"So you two seem to be getting along well," Trish smirked, keeping her voice low enough so only I could hear.

I took the last tile from the box and laid it in place. "What can I say," I began, "he's easy to get along with. I'm just waiting for the other foot to fall."

"What's that supposed to mean?"

"Well, he's a little too perfect. There has to be a catch." I stood up and stretched, my legs had grown stiff from kneeling so long. "I'm just saying, I wouldn't be surprised if one day he stopped talking to me or something."

"No way," Trish mumbled, "I don't see that happening." Trish had never been the dating type, I couldn't remember her having a boyfriend for as long as we'd known each other. For her to be this interested in my…love life…it had me puzzled.

"I told him about the stolen dogs," I admitted.

"You must like him an awful lot to reveal such important information." She extended a hand as a cue for me to help her up. "I think you guys would make an excellent couple."

"Maybe he just wants to be my friend," I said quietly as we made our way to the room next to the one he was working on. "It probably won't even go anywhere."

"I think your wrong," she smirked, ending the conversation. "Hand me a box of tiles and let's wrap this up, my body is killing from all this manual labor you are having me do."

Eric peeked in just as we finished talking about him and scared us half to death. "How are you ladies coming along?" he laughed seeing us both jump.

"Just getting started on this one," I replied, still laughing. "Is the last suite done?"

"It is," he bragged, "what's the hold up? I figured you would be waiting on me, not the other way around." Narrowing his eyes, he gave a joking tisk tisk and walked away with a box of tiles.

"Go help him," Trish persuaded, "I've got this one under control."

Hesitantly, I stood up and dusted myself off before joining Eric in the next room over. Looking up at me, he smiled and asked what I needed.

"Trish kicked me out, said I was holding her up," I joked. "Care if I join you?"

"Oh, I don't know," he laughed, handing me a stack of tiles. "Only if you promise not to slow me down."

"I can't make any promises, but I'll try to keep up!"

Surprisingly, Trish finished before us and poked her head in to let me know she was heading home for the night. "See you in the morning," she chirped, flashing me a smile.

"What was that about?" Eric laughed once she was gone.

"What was what about?" I smiled, knowing exactly what he meant.

"She is always sending you sly little smiles, like she has a secret," he pointed out. "What are you hiding?"

"I'm not hiding anything," I confirmed, taking the last tile out of his hand and placing it neatly amongst the rest. "She just has this crazy idea."

"Idea?" he asked hesitantly. "What kind of idea?"

"Oh, it's nothing," I assured him. "Just Trish being silly."

"Now I'm curious," he pushed. "Spill."

"She just thinks that we would make a cute couple," I laughed, looking down embarrassedly.

"Oh does she?"

"I guess," I replied. "Hey, do you have time to help me with Jaxx before you leave?"

"It's my night off, I have all the time you need," he smiled, going along with my attempt to change the subject.

"Well if that's the case," I joked, "I have a whole room that needs to be set up to live in."

"Whatever you need help with, just let me know," he replied seriously. "If you want me to stay and help set up your new apartment I would be more than happy to."

"That would help a lot," I thanked him as we made our way to Jaxx's kennel.

It was a beautiful night to go for a walk, so we made the most of it and took several dogs after out after Jaxx. Taking Reina and Ace out last, I explained her past and how she was the dog I had wanted him to adopt the first time we met.

"She wasn't good around the other dogs when I first got her here," I explained. "It hasn't taken long for her to warm up to Ace and Posh though."

"Maybe I can bring my boy over one night soon and see how she does with him," he suggested, bending down to pet Reina before we took them back inside. "He is really calm, I bet they would do great together."

"That would be awesome!" I agreed, "I really want to get her out of here, she deserves a great home with all the bad she has been put through."

"If you're not busy tomorrow, I can bring him by in the morning," he beamed, clearly excited to add another dog to his family. "Of course, that is if you want me to."

"Yea! That would be great," I replied, hoping the two would get along perfectly and she could go to a real home.

Having gotten all the dogs out for the first time in a few days, I felt a wave of contentment wash over me as we began setting up the room I chose to make my apartment. It was big enough to put my own private bathroom in, as well as a small kitchen. Even though it wasn't much, I felt more at home than I had at my actual house.

"You're really ok with living in a warehouse?" Eric laughed, unaware of just how excited I was to move in.

"Actually, I think I am," I replied happily. Visualizing in my head how I wanted the layout to look, I smiled.

"You seem genuinely happy right now," he pointed out. "What are you thinking?"

"There's a lot on my mind," I replied. Leaving it at that, I pointed to where I wanted my kitchen to be built and how I wanted an open floor concept like a studio apartment.

"I think it's going to be perfect for you," he admitted.

After moving the furniture around, several times, I finally settled with where they were and flopped down on the couch. Checking my phone, I gasped at the time.

"It's almost two in the morning!" I choked. "I can't believe how late it is."

"That's weird, I'm not even tired," he replied causally.

"I'm really not all that tired either," I admitted. "I mean my body is exhausted, but I'm not tired."

"Well, if you want me to get going just say the word," he said, sitting down next to me on the only piece of furniture I had. "Or, since neither of us are tired, we could bring a few dogs in here and watch a movie with them. You know, to get them out of their kennels."

"Yea, we could do that," I laughed, pushing aside his adorable attempt to make it seem like it was in the dogs best interest that we watched a movie. "I'll grab Ace and Posh if you want to get Reina. We can really make it a party and add Mia to the pack as well. I know she gets along with my two, but I would like to see how she and Reina do together."

After laying a pile of blankets down on the floor in front of the couch, we gathered all the dogs and met back in the room to see how they all got along. Leaving Reina on a leash in case something went wrong, I kept her close to me while everyone else sniffed around. I could tell she was a little tense, with so many dogs around and in a new setting I couldn't blame her. Ace jumped up on the couch next to me, gave a quick lick on the face and laid down. To my surprise, Reina climbed up next to her and let out a deep sigh of contentment. She was clearly the most comfortable when the big husky was around. Before long we had all four dogs up on the couch, smooshing Eric and I together in the middle.

"Isn't this something!" he laughed, "I wish my guy was here to join in on all the fun."

"He is welcome any time," I said, getting up to turn on the TV. Thanks to Ace, I had no remote controller and had to do everything manually. Looking back to where my spot on the couch was, I laughed when I saw that it gotten considerably smaller. Trying to squeeze into the little space I had left, I ended up more in Eric's lap than I did on the couch. "Sorry," I laughed, "they're not much for personal space as you can see!"

"I'm not complaining," he replied, a smile creeping across his face. Moving his arm so I could lean back, he causally draped it across my shoulder, sending goosebumps down my arms. I could definitely get used to ending my long, hectic days like this.

About halfway through the movie, I finally felt my body relax. It was awkward sitting so close to him at first, but after a while it felt as though we had been doing this forever. Leaning my head against his shoulder, I felt his arm tighten around me pulling me closer, and I couldn't help but smile. We sat this way until the movie ended and the credits had run through, all that was left on the television was a black screen.

"I should probably get heading home," he whispered.

"Yeah," I agreed, forcing myself to get up. I just wanted to stay that way all night, but I knew he had his dog to get home to. "Are you still planning on coming over tomorrow, well today I guess it would be?"

"Of course," he smiled. "I'll be back after I get a few hours of sleep." Making his way through the pack of dogs, he finally reached the door and wished me a good night.

"Goodnight," I smiled back.

For the first time in over a week, I finally had a bed to sleep in. There was no better feeling than sinking into a nice soft mattress after sleeping on the hard ground for so long. Remembering I had four dogs that would soon realize this too, I quickly pulled the blankets over me just as they all began swarming my bed. Ace, never being one to hesitate on a comfortable spot to lay, was the first to jump up and claim the pillow next to me. Rolling over to put my arm around him like I always did, I felt the remaining three pile around me as I closed my eyes and gave in to exhaustion.

Having actually gone to sleep at a reasonable hour, it was no surprise that Trish, being the morning person she was, arrived before I rolled out of bed.

"Someone stayed up past their bedtime," she laughed, walking into my room and setting the dogs off into a frenzy of barking. "Get up! We have work to do."

"I'm up," I yawned, still half asleep. "It better not be no six o'clock in the morning."

"Try ten o'clock," she replied as she yanked my covers off. "The dogs are starving, and the kennels aren't going to clean themselves!"

Forcing myself out of bed, I threw on a pair of old jeans and a hoodie, then returned the dogs to their new private rooms. The kennel already seemed to be a much more peaceful environment, as dogs weren't raging at each other in frustration waiting for their breakfast. Finding Trish in the adjoining room, I set out the food bowls as she filled them with food.

"So," Trish began, filling the last of the bowls, "what kept you up all night?"

"We watched a movie after getting all the dogs out for a walk," I smiled innocently.

"Is he coming over today?" she asked as we began setting the food in front of each of the rooms.

"Yeah," I giggled, kind of embarrassed at how excited I felt. "He is bringing his dog Kado, over to see if Reina gets along with him."

"So he is really considering adopting her?"

"I think he really wants her, but ultimately it's up to Reina." I wasn't going to force the dog into a situation that would make her uncomfortable. Even if it took several meet and greets with Eric's dog, we would take it slow and make sure it was a good match.

Once all the bowls of food were placed in front of the rooms, we made our way back up the line and pushed them in. The way we built the front of the suites, with the gate a few inches off the ground, made it a lot easier than having to open every door and fight our way in. Mornings were always the most hectic, as the dogs were restless and hungry.

"Well I hope it all works out for her," Trish smiled as she pushed Reina's breakfast in to her room. "She deserves a good home."

"I hope so too," I replied.

Waiting for the dogs to finish before we began cleaning, I sat down in one of the chairs we had salvaged and began running some numbers. With the cost of building the suites, and remodeling the play room, after I put in a kitchen and bathroom to make my apartment complete, there wouldn't be much money left.

"So I was thinking," I began, motioning Trish to come over. "What if we host some kind of benefit to raise money for the rescue?"

Trish loved planning parties, so I wasn't surprised when her face lit up. "What kind of benefit?" she asked excitedly.

"Well, I was thinking something that would attract all of our rich friends back home, as well as the upper class people in Atlanta. Maybe something like a ball, where everyone could enjoy an evening out and get dressed up. How often, besides prom, do people get to wear fancy dresses and get all done up?"

"I like where this is going," she grinned. "We could set up a stage, and introduce all of the dogs to get them exposure as well. Not only could it raise money, but maybe we could get a few of the dogs homes as well!"

"That's a really good idea," I thought out loud. "We could have fancy catering and a band come in, and do some raffles or a silent auction."

"Say no more!" she chirped. "I'm all over it! Give me a spending limit and I will have it planned and invitations sent out. When are you wanting to have it?"

"The sooner the better," I replied, glad to see her excited and taking control. She had always done all my party planning back home, and never once disappointed me. I always told her she should have been a wedding planner or event coordinator.

"I'll have it planned in no time," she smiled.

We were still talking party ideas when Eric showed up and let himself in. "Hey stranger," he called as he walked toward us.

"Hey!" I gushed back. Realizing the level of excitement behind my tone, I dialed it back a little. "Where's your little guy?"

"He's still in the truck," he replied, "I wasn't sure where you wanted to do the meet and greet at."

"She seems to be most comfortable when she is walked with another dog first, so why don't you grab him and we can all go for a quick loop around the block to let them get familiar with each other. Then we can head over to the play room if everything goes well and see how they do in there," I instructed.

"Sounds like a plan. I'll grab him and meet you out front," he replied excitedly.

Trish leashed up Reina while I searched for the box of treats. I had been reading a lot of dog training articles online in my free time, and one of the trainers I really liked used something called positive reinforcement training. I tried following their method with Reina every chance I got, and it seemed to really make a difference.

As soon as we got outside, Reina caught sight of Kado and immediately stiffened. I yelled for him to stay there for a minute, while I got Reina to focus on me instead of the other dog. The second she turned her attention to me, I quickly handed out a treat. Every step we took closer, I would reward her for staying calm. She was a really fast learner, so it didn't take long to get her comfortable in the presence of the strange dog.

"Put him on your left side," I told Eric, after positioning Trish in between us. Keeping Reina on my side furthest away from Eric and Kado, we began our walk down the street. For being in the middle of the city, the road the facility was on seemed to remain fairly quiet for the most part. Taking advantage of the lack of traffic, we spread ourselves out and gave the dogs plenty of space to create a comfortable atmosphere. Slowly drawing them closer together, by the time we returned to the warehouse they were walking only a few feet apart with no problem.

Finally, we put some slack in the leashes and allowed the two dogs to greet each other. I was a little hesitant, but I felt her body language was telling me she was comfortable so I followed my gut and tried to remain calm as they sniffed one another curiously. At first Reina was uncertain, keeping her tail tucked slightly under her body, but as soon as Kado gave a play bow her entire demeanor changed. I smiled seeing the frightened dog begin wiggling and dancing around like a puppy.

"I think she found a boyfriend," Trish laughed. "I've never seen her act like that with any of the other dogs."

"Me either!" I agreed, overjoyed that the two dogs were getting along so well. "Let's go ahead and take them in the play room and see how they do. Keep his leash on though, we want to be able to separate them if things escalade."

Watching Reina run and play with another dog made my heart dance. I didn't think she would ever be the same dog as she was before the neighbors took her, but she was getting there. Seeing her now, you would never believe she was used as bait.

"What do you think, boss?" Eric laughed, "Are they a good match or what!"

"I think we should do this another time or two before she goes home with you, but it definitely looks promising," I smiled.

"Your just saying that so I have to come back," he joked, lightly bumping me with his arm.

"You caught me," I laughed.

"I don't have much planned today if you need help with anything," he informed me as we picked up the leashes after a good hour of watching them play.

"Well," I began, "I need to get this room finished as soon as possible. Trish and I are planning on hosting an event here to raise money for the rescue, and this is the biggest room so I would like to have it in here. I had originally planned on putting in artificial grass, but I think I'll just go with rubber matting. I want to paint all the walls as well, just to make it look nicer."

"Do you have the flooring yet?" he asked, probably wondering how I could afford all of this remodeling.

"I placed the order, but it won't be delivered for a few more days. I figured it would be better to get the walls painted first anyway, just in case paint gets spilled or something."

"Let's get to painting then," Eric smiled. "Do you have somewhere I can put Kado while we work?"

"I can move some dogs around and free up one of the suites," I replied, thinking of who got along the best together. "Go ahead and put him in Mia's room, I'll stick her in the apartment with Posh and Ace."

The room was a lot bigger than I thought, and I hadn't bought enough paint to finish so we all piled into Eric's SUV and made our way to the hardware store.

"So what kind of event are you planning on having?" Eric asked, after we had checked out and were loading the paint into the back.

"I don't know what I'm going to call it yet, but basically it's going to be like an adult prom. A black tie and formal dress event with good food and a silent auction or raffle, and of course dancing.

"Well that sounds like a really good time, am I invited?" he joked, shooting me a puppy dog face.

"Only if you attend as my date," I joked back. "I'm just kidding, of course your invited. I won't even charge you the admission fee."

This earned a laugh from both Eric and Trish.

"What can I do to help?" Eric asked. "If you print up flyers I can hand them out at the station. I'm sure all the officers wives would love to attend."

"I will have flyers ready in no time," Trish piped in from the back seat. "As soon as Karen gives me a date and budget I will begin planning everything."

"I don't mean to sound rude," Eric began, "but how can you afford to put on this kind of event. Don't it cost a lot of money for something like this?"

I figured he would catch on sooner or later and ask where all the money was coming from, so I had already came up with an answer ahead of time. "My parents are going to loan me the money, and I will pay them back after the event."

"Well that is nice of them to do," he replied. "I didn't get the impression that you had a very good relationship with them from what I saw at the hospital."

"My mom was just mad," I lied. I honestly had hardly any relationship with her, but my dad and I had always been close.

"That's understandable." He laughed. "I don't know what I would do if my daughter got into trouble and ended up at the hospital.

The whole vehicle instantly got quiet, as what he said lingered in the air. Finally, figuring I wasn't going to say anything, Trish spoke up.

"Wait, you have a daughter?" she questioned, shooting me a look of surprise.

Eric was silent for few moments longer before finally answering. "I do," he admitted. "I didn't want to say anything before getting to know you Karen. I don't like to bring her around new relationships, only to have her heartbroken when they don't work out. I'm sorry for keeping it a secret. I hope it isn't a deal breaker."

I could hardly be mad, as I had a handful of my own secrets I was keeping from him. I didn't know what to say though. I wasn't upset, but I didn't know the first thing about kids.

"How old is she?" I finally asked.

"Her name is Abby and she is eleven," he replied, glancing from the road to look at me to see my reaction.

"Eleven?" I reiterated, "how old are you?" I guess I had never asked his age before, as I figured he was in his mid to late twenties like myself.

"Thirty-one," he answered, looking my way again. "I was just starting police academy just when she was born."

At least she wasn't a baby, I thought to myself. The thought of having a little kid around scared me. I must had missed the baby fever every girl my age goes through, as I never had any desire to have any of my own. I could probably handle an eleven year old though.

"Is that a problem?" Eric asked hesitantly, after I didn't respond.

"No, it's not a problem," I replied quickly, realizing I was off in la la land and hadn't said anything in a while. "Does she live with you then, or do you have shared custody?"

"I have full custody of her," he explained. "Sharon, her mom, didn't want anything to do with having kids after she got married a few years ago. It started out with joint custody, then when Abby turned six my ex gave me full custody."

"Wow," I gasped, surprised that someone could give up their kid like that. I didn't even particularly like kids and I didn't think that was something I could ever do.

"Yea, thankfully my mother helps me with watching her when I work…"

"Or come over here," I interrupted, instantly feeling bad for taking up so much of his time.

"She doesn't mind, she stops over all the time and says she is taking Abby for the weekend. They go on little trips together and have fun."

The rest of the drive back to the warehouse was silent and slightly awkward. I didn't really know what to say, since I wasn't sure how I felt about the whole situation. I really liked the guy, and he was by far the nicest out of all the men I had hung out with, but I didn't know how I felt about dating someone with a kid that was almost half my age.

"Can we talk for a minute?" Eric asked once we pulled into the parking lot.

Taking this as her cue to leave, Trish quickly got out and said she would get started painting and give us some time alone.

"What is going through your mind?" he asked, looking at me concerned. "Is that too much for you? Is it the age difference, or the having a kid part?"

"It isn't that big of an age difference," I began, trying to get my thoughts together. "I guess I've just never been around kids so I don't know how to feel about it." Seeing the look on his face broke my heart. I could tell he really liked me and didn't want this to end. In that moment I made up my mind. Guys like him didn't come around every day, and I wasn't going to let something so insignificant push me away. At my age, I would be lucky to find a guy who didn't already have children.

Before I could put my thoughts into words, Eric grabbed ahold of my hand and told me that other than his daughter, I had become the most important person in his life, and that he hadn't felt like this about any other girl he had ever dated.

Sitting there a moment, I let his words sink in. "I don't want this to end," I finally whispered. "It's been over a year since I've even gone on a date with anyone, you were the first guy that has been able to take my focus off work and the rescue since I began doing it."

I could hear him let out a relieved breath, as he must have been holding it waiting for my response. "You don't know how happy that makes me hearing you say that," he smiled. Getting out of the vehicle, he made his way over to the passenger side and opened my door. Taking my hand in his, he helped me out and wrapped his arms around me, burring my face in his chest.

Out of all the guys I'd dated in my past, not a single one of them made me feel the way I did right now. I knew in that moment, I was completely head over heels in love with this man. There was nothing I could think of that would cause me to run away from this, and I was glad I had come to my senses before it was too late.

Feeling his arms loosen, I was about to look up when I felt his lips gently place a kiss on my forehead. I had never believed in the whole weak in the knees concept, until now, as I had to grab ahold of his arm to keep myself from going down.

"You alright?" he asked, obliviously. "Do you need to sit down?"

Laughing, I told him I was fine. "We should really get in there and help Trish finish painting."

"You're probably right," he replied reluctantly.

As I turned to head into the warehouse, he grabbed my hand and spun me around so I was face to face with him. Before I had a chance to say anything, he took my face in his hands and leaned down to kiss me. It wasn't a quick kiss either, but rather hungry and full of passion, like he had been waiting for this moment for a long time.

"I'm sorry," he apologized after finally pulling himself away. "You don't know how long I've wanted to do that."

"Don't apologize," I smiled, after catching my breath. "I've been wanting you to do that since the day we met."

"You too?" he laughed.

"Yeah," I began. "I think at first it was because I found you extremely good looking, but after spending time with you I think it gradually became a different reason."

"Like what?" he teased, kissing me once again. This time it was short and sweet, as if to prove a point.

"I don't know," I lied, not wanting to rush into saying that I loved him. I was fairly positive that I did, but it had only been a few weeks and I just thought that was too soon to say it.

"Tell me," he whispered gently, still holding my face in his hands.

"I think you already know," I replied, searching his crystal blue eyes for some sign that he felt the same.

"I know it has only been a short time that we've known each other," he began, knowing exactly what I was thinking, "but I think I'm falling in love with you."

"I think I'm falling in love with you too," I whispered back.

Having lost all motivation to get any work done, we stood there and embraced each other for a while longer, soaking in the moment. I could hear his heart beating as I rested my head gently against his chest. I imagine we would have stayed in that position for a lot longer, had Trish not walked out and interrupted the moment.

Quickly stepping away from him, I called over to her that we were on our way in. Before I could say anymore, I saw her smile and disappear back into the building.

"Well that was awkward," I laughed.

"She's the one who said we would make a cute couple," he joked back. "We should get in there and help though, before I steal you away." Taking ahold of my hand, he lead the way inside.

"How nice of you to join me," Trish announced as we walked into the room. "I was beginning to think I would be finishing this all on my own."

Grabbing my brush out of the can of paint, I stuck my finger into the white liquid and dabbed it on her nose. Before she could get me back, I took off across the room and shot her a playful smile. "Still glad to have us back?" I giggled.

Feeling something cold brush against my cheek, I spun around and saw Eric standing there with a grin on his face and a white finger.

"Don't worry Trish, I got her back," he chuckled.

"Oh, it's on now," I sneered as I drew the dripping paint brush from the can. It was a good thing we decided to do the floor last, as things were about to get messy.

Before long, the three of us were speckled head to toe in white paint, laying on the floor laughing like a bunch of kids. I couldn't remember the last time I had this much fun.

"I have an idea," I blurted out as a thought popped into my head. "White walls are so boring, and I want this place to be full of life. Why don't we get some bring colored paint, and after they're all finished being painted white, we can do some kind of splatter design with all the colors!"

"I think that would be fun," Trish agreed. "Would definitely bring some life to this old room."

"I can pick up some more paint before I come over tomorrow evening," Eric added. "I have to get heading out soon though, and we should probably finish painting the rest so it has the night to dry."

Everyone was getting ready to leave when Eric asked if it would be okay if he brought his daughter over to help tomorrow.

"I think she would have fun slinging paint around with us, and it would be a good way to introduce you two," he suggested. "That's only if you're ready though."

"That's a good idea," I replied, still nervous about meeting his daughter.

After saying our goodbyes, I went to my apartment to get cleaned up before beginning evening chores.

CHAPTER 6

Fighting back nerves as I waited for Eric and his daughter to arrive, I decided to start working on Reina's leash manners to distract myself. Lately on her walks I had noticed her to be pulling more and more, and I wanted to break the habit before it turned into a problem so I leashed her and Ace up to begin the training session. Since Ace walked so calmly, despite her energetic personality, I decided to try walking them together to see if it would persuade Reina to walk better to stay next to her favorite companion.

"Easy girl," I told the hyper dog as she began prancing around, pulling at the leash. Ace had already fell into perfect stride next to me, and curiously watched as Reina wandered all over. Looping the lead several times to draw her closer, I watched as the hyper dog struggled to get ahead of us with her nose to the ground taking every scent in.

Thankful Ace was on her best behavior, I focused on trying to get Reina's attention on me. Remembering I had put a few treats in my pocket earlier that morning, I dug one out and broke it in half, giving one to Ace and using the other to lure the distracted Reina closer to me. As soon as she switched her focus from sniffing the ground to paying attention to me, I quickly handed her the treat and told her good girl. Before she had finished chewing the biscuit, she went right back to pulling me around. Frustrated that my idea of using Ace had failed, I turned the two dogs around and headed back to the warehouse to begin getting ready for the eventful day ahead of me.

Trish arrived an hour earlier than expected, so we sat down and began some event planning, for what we had decided to call the Four Paws Royal Gala. Having already started working on it, Trish presented me with a layout design she had drawn up, showing how the floorplan would look. Along with her, by no means novice, sketches, she had also saved the websites to several catering companies as well as table and chair rentals.

"I think since we are going to go for a bright and lively theme for this room, the event should mirror it and be equally as colorful. What do you think about these?" She asked, handing me her phone. Swiping through the pictures she had saved of different color themes, I narrowed it down to the three I liked best.

"I really like this one," I replied, after looking through them once more. Round tables adorned with vibrant purple tablecloths were strategically placed around the room, joined with chairs covered in a white fabric cover with silver sashes. There were nets draped from the ceiling with millions of lights, causing it to look like the event was being held under the starts.

"We could definitely pull something like this off," Trish squeaked excitedly, clearly enjoying her role as event coordinator. "I also sent out emails to several companies who matched you with local bands in the area, telling them we needed one that would play only instrumental as it was for an dinner party and not a rave."

"Should we have a DJ for later, after the dinner?" I asked.

"Well of course," she laughed, "I already have that covered though. One of the girls I go to school with, her boyfriend has all the equipment and does a lot of gigs in Atlanta. I told her about the event, and she said he would do it for free if we gave her tickets for her and a friend."

"I guess that's covered then!" I laughed, amazed at Trish's bargaining skills.

"So you still haven't given me a budget to work with," she reminded. "I can't officially start planning and get things rolling without knowing how much I am able to spend."

"Would ten thousand get us everything we need?" I asked, completely clueless as to how much something like this would cost to put on.

"It depends, how many tickets do you want to sell. Catering will probably be the biggest expense, so I need an idea of how many people will be attending," she pointed out.

"How many people do you think this room can hold?"

I watched her look around, carefully evaluating the unfinished, half painted room. "Do you know how many square feet this room is?" she finally asked.

Having just ordered the flooring for it, I racked my brain trying to remember the dimensions of the room. "I believe it was 120 by 80," I replied, whipping out my phone to punch the numbers into the calculator. "So 9600 square feet."

Smiling, Trish did something on her phone and then told me it would fit about 800 guests if we did a round table banquet style event.

"How did you figure that out?" I laughed.

"I have an app on my phone for party planning," she replied casually, like that was something everyone had readily available.

"Only you would have something like that," I joked. "Does that include a dance floor and stage area?"

"No, we would have to figure out how much room we want the dining area to be and that would give us the most accurate approximation of how many guests we can comfortably hold," she answered. Pointing to her drawing, she showed where the stage and dance floor would be as well as an area with tables for a silent auction. I also thought we could do a kissing booth and use one or two of the dogs. I've seen a lot of shelters do it at fundraising events and it looks like a lot of fun. Plus it would get even more exposure for the dogs."

"That would be the perfect job for Tank," I laughed. "He can't keep his tongue in his mouth as it is, might as well get paid for all his kisses."

Looking at the drawing, we figured out the sizes of all the areas and decided to set the ticket sale at $50. If we could sell all 500 tickets, the event would raise $25,000, plus whatever the auction brought in as well as donations.

We were still event planning when Ace ran over and started barking at the door before I heard a faint knock. It never amazed me at how well they could hear.

"Eric must be here," I looked at Trish anxiously. All the event planning had taken my mind off of meeting his daughter for the first time and now it was all hitting me at once causing a knot to form in my stomach.

"Hey beautiful," he smiled as I opened the door and let him in. Giving me a quick kiss on the cheek, he looked back to his suburban and said Abby was getting something out for me.

"For me?" I asked confused, wondering if I should have gotten her something as well. I didn't even know what Eric had told her about me. Were we just friends? Was I her dads new girlfriend? I didn't exactly know where we stood myself to be honest.

"Well, for the dogs I should say," he replied. "She spent all evening baking treats for them."

"That was sweet of her," I smiled. I didn't know eleven year old's could bake, but then again I had no idea of what age could do what since I had never been around kids.

"She is very....mature, for her age," he confirmed without me having to say anything. "She also loves dogs, so I think you two are really going to hit it off."

Hearing the vehicle door slam, I waited next to Eric with Ace at my side. As soon as the husky caught sight of the little girl, she took off running toward her so fast it made gravel go flying under her feet.

"Ace!" I yelled, taking off after her. I had no idea how she was around kids, and every worse case scenario came rushing into my head all at once. By the time I reached them, Ace had the little girl knocked down on the ground, and to my relief, was showering her in doggy kisses. I didn't know anything about her past, before I adopted her, but based on the fact that there was an open container of dog cookies laying on the ground next to Abby, and her complete focus remained on the little girl, gave me an indication that she had been in a home with kids before.

Relieved when I heard Eric's daughter giggling from beneath the mountain of fur that was smothering her, I looked up at Eric and smiled.

"I told you she loves dogs," he laughed.

"Come on Ace," I said, pulling the dog off of her. The husky looked up at me with what I could have sworn was the happiest face I had ever seen her have.

"I like her," Abby chirped, picking up the container of cookies. "Can I give her one?"

"Of course," I smiled.

Watching how gentle she took the cookie from the little girl, it confirmed my thoughts that she had been around kids before. Ace was normally a piranha when it came to taking treats from anyone.

"Do you want to see the rest of the dogs?" I asked, feeling more comfortable than I thought I would.

"YES!" She replied excitedly, taking her dads hand and pulling him toward the building.

"Lead the way," Eric told me, a smile creeping over his face.

We made our way through the room as Abby handed out cookies to all the dogs, then turned around and she gave them all seconds.

"Which one are we taking home?" She asked her dad.

Eric took her back over to Reina's suite and pointed to the little brown pit bull. "This one will hopefully be our new addition. What do you think?"

"I like her!" she squealed. "I like Ace too though. Can we take them both?"

"Ace is Karen's dog," he explained. "She would be really sad if we took her."

I laughed. "Her sister would miss her a lot too."

"She has a sister? Where is she?" Abby questioned, running from one room to the next looking inside.

I lead the way to my apartment and opened the door for Posh to come out. "This is her sister, Posh," I laughed.

"They don't look like sisters," the little girl replied, confused. "They don't look anything alike."

"Well they're not actually sisters," Eric told her. "They're both Karen's dogs though, so it kind of makes them sisters don't you think?"

"Yea, I suppose." She extended her hand toward Posh, and let the little beagle sniff it. "Oh yea, here's a cookie for you!"

After playing with Posh and Ace awhile longer, we threw on some old t-shirts and made our way to the room we had started painting. The idea was to splatter different color paints all over the walls, to bring life to the plain white room. Trish had shot me a text saying she was running late, and to get started without her, so I opened the cans of paint and had Abby pick out her favorite color.

"She'll choose pink," Eric whispered to me as we watched her look from one paint can to the next. "That's her favorite color. She has always been a little bit of a girly girl."

"Hey!" I laughed, poking him in the side. "There is nothing wrong with being a girly girl."

Hearing us both laughing, Abby looked over and asked what was so funny, as she picked up the can of pink paint.

"Nothing," Eric replied. "We were just guessing which color you were going to pick."

Once we had all picked out a color we began the art of paint slinging. I wasn't sure that was the actual term for what we were doing, but that's what Abby said it was so we went along with it. Looking at the floor, I was certainly glad we decided to do this before installing the new mats as there was more paint on the concrete than on the walls.

We were having so much fun, I didn't hear Trish enter the building until she was right behind me. "You guys having fun without me!" she chirped.

"We're having a blast," I laughed. "There's another can of paint if you want to grab it and help us. You should probably change out of your good clothes too."

Deciding to take a break while waiting for Trish to return, we followed Abby into the main kennel area after she asked if it would be alright if she gave the dogs all another treat. Watching her face light up at each room, my mind began to change towards how I felt about Eric having a kid. I guess all the kids I had ever been around, were rich California brats who had no manners and expected everything. Abby, for being only eleven years old, was really smart as well as well mannered. I could see us becoming good friends if things continued to go the way they were with her dad.

"After we're done painting, can we take Reina out for a walk?" she asked me, instead of her dad.

"Sure," I smiled. "You can help me feed them too if you'd like."

"Yes!" she exclaimed, jumping up and down excitedly.

By the time we finished painting the room, it was well past the dogs dinner time and I could hear howling coming from the other room as the they announced their disapproval of my tardiness. Keeping my promise, I let Abby fill their food bowls as I told her how much to put in each one, and then we handed them out together while Eric and Trish cleaned up the paint supplies. Just as we finished sliding the bowls in to their hungry owners, Eric strolled up with a grin on his face.

"What's up?" I asked curiously, wondering what was going on.

"Nothing," he replied, still smiling ear to ear. "It's just nice to see you two getting along so well."

"Did you think we wouldn't?"

"She didn't exactly get along with last girl I dated. She was okay with her at first, but after a while I think she began to get jealous."

"Do you think she will be like that with me?" I could understand where she was coming from, I would get jealous too if it was usually just me and my dad and all of a sudden someone else was getting all his attention.

"I honestly don't think so," he paused, obviously deep in thought. "You two have a lot in common and I think, especially with being able to help you with the dogs, she will see you more as a friend than someone she has to compete with for my attention."

I really liked Eric, so I was relieved to hear him say that he thought everything would be ok between me and his daughter, especially with her prior behavior toward ex-girlfriends. Every relationship I had been in back in California was short lived and pointless, more or less just something to pass the time. It was different with Eric, however. I actually wanted to be with him, and not just for what he could offer me. For the first time in my life, I was actually going to give a relationship a real shot.

"I'll be honest with you," I looked around to make sure Abby wasn't within hearing distance, " I wasn't sure how I felt about you having a kid. Now that I've met her though, I think I will really enjoy having her around."

I could see how happy it made him to hear that. I knew his daughter would always come first, as she should, so I could imagine what a relief it was to see us getting along so well.

I was about to say something, but Abby walked back over before I got the chance. Changing the subject I asked if she was ready to take Reina out for her walk and possibly, if her dad was okay with it, stop for ice cream while we were out.

Taking advantage of all the bodies, I paired everyone up with a dog to take to the ice cream shop down the road. Since Abby was small, I let her walk Posh while Eric walked Reina and Kado. Trish took Ace and Mia, since they walked really well together, and I grabbed Shay. It had been awhile since I'd gotten the chance to work with her around other dogs, and this made the perfect opportunity for a training session. Shay was the other female pit that showed up at my house with Mia after escaping from the neighbor's property. It wasn't surprising that she had a small degree of dog aggression, coming from the situation she was put in.

I let Trish lead the way while I hung back with Shay, rewarding her for staying calm and relaxed around the group of dog ahead. Slowly, I closed the gap and brought her up next to Ace and Mia, never pushing her to get to close to where she wasn't comfortable. The idea was to make her realize that being around other dogs would get her a reward, thus making it a positive experience. This method had worked great with Reina when she first came back and was nervous around other dogs.

After ordering our ice cream, I got five doggie bowls and we all sat down at the picnic table and enjoyed our afternoon treat. I watched as the dogs contently lapped up their little bowl of ice cream, and wished I could bring them all here every day.

It was late by the time we got back, and after getting the dogs to their rooms we said our goodbyes and everyone went their separate ways.

Having gotten used to being off the past few days, it was harder than usual getting out of bed for work when my alarm went off. Finally, after hitting snooze more times than I should have, I looked at my phone and realized I was running half an hour behind and still had to feed all the dogs. Jumping out of bed I quickly threw some clothes on and rushed into the kennel to begin getting the food ready. It would be nice to have help in the mornings, especially on the days I had to work.

Once the dogs were fed and taken out to go the bathroom, I finished getting ready and grabbed my lunch before heading to my car. Speeding the entire way there, I made it in record time and clocked in at exactly eight o'clock.

"Running late this morning?" Elaine asked, before catching me up on what I had missed on my days off.

Hearing we were at full capacity did nothing to improve my morning. I didn't have the time at the moment to take in more dogs, but it was looking like I would have to make some. I hoped this event would result in at least a few dogs getting adopted, so I had room for more when I needed it.

"Which dogs are on the euthanasia list this week?" I asked as we made our way through the kennel. Each dog had an intake paper attached to the front of their kennel, and I skimmed over the new ones as we passed by.

"Zoro and Zelda, the two pit mixes that came in together two weeks ago are both on it." She paused to think of the rest of the names. It was hard to keep all the dogs straight as we went through so many of them here, but we did make an effort to give every one of them a name. Neither of us liked the idea of referring to any living creature as kennel number. "The little white terrier mix is on it as well. I can't think of the other two off the top of my head."

I was surprised the terrier hadn't found a home yet since small dogs were usually the first to get adopted. She was a really sweet dog and as far as I knew her only problem was she pulled hard on the leash. It would be nice if we had enough staff to free up some time to do training, but that wasn't the case.

"Where's Annie?" I asked after once we had reached the end of the building and I hadn't seen her in the mix.

"I put a crate in the break room," she explained, "during the day she stays in there.

"Is she ok?" I immediately assumed something was wrong as the only time we moved dogs out of the kennel was when they were ill or showing signs of extreme stress.

"She's shut right down," Elaine responded hesitantly. "We've tried to get her to eat, this will be her third day with no food."

Walking into the break room, I prepared myself for the worse. The crate sat in the back with a blanket draped over all but the front of it, and as I quietly lifted the corner she raised her head and looked at me with the saddest eyes I had ever seen. My heart shattered.

CHAPTER 7

It had been almost a week since I was approved to foster Annie and she had already made an incredible amount of progress since being released from the shelter. Two days after arriving at the warehouse, she was still barely eating so I decided to put a crate in my apartment instead of leaving her alone in one of the suites. Having other dogs around, not in a noisy shelter atmosphere, must had made her feel comfortable since the morning after moving her in with Ace and Posh, she finally ate all her breakfast.

It has been several days since then and her appetite was still thriving. Every morning she got a special breakfast consisting of kibble and eggs along with some cooked chicken I had made earlier in the week. Fearing my dogs would get jealous, they each got an egg mixed in with their food as well.

Just as I was getting ready to clean the kennels out, Eric and Abby showed up for a surprise visit, each carrying a large box in their arms. Looking inside as they set them on the floor, I saw neatly folded blankets in one and toys in the other

"I told all my friends at school to bring in supplies to donate to a dog rescue," Abby informed me with a smile.

Eric turned to his daughter and told her to tell me what else she said to her friends. Looking up at me he shook his head, waiting for Abby to tell the rest of the story.

"I told them if they didn't bring anything in, my daddy was going to arrest them."

"What!" I laughed. "You did not say that!"

"I sure did," she replied confidently. "It worked didn't it!"

I didn't know what to say. Maybe I should put her in charge of selling tickets to the event. "I can't believe you said that."

"Well, you mentioned the other day that you had brought four more dogs in, so I figured you would need all the help you could get." She handed me an envelope then took off to visit with the dogs.

"What's this?" I looked at Eric and quickly came to the conclusion that he didn't have a clue. Opening the envelope, I found several five dollar bills and a gift card to a feed store in Atlanta.

"Abby, where did this money come from?" He yelled for her to come back over.

"Dad, its fine," she said, dismissing his attempt to talk to her. "It's just some of my friends lunch money their parents sent them."

Returning her focus on Reina, she slipped her a cookie under the door and headed for the next suite.

"I don't know what I'm going to do with her," he sighed. "Ever since meeting you, all she talks about is rescuing dogs and coming over here to help."

"Is that a bad thing?" I laughed, gently punching him in the arm. "It could be a whole lot worse. She's almost to the boy crazy age, then you're really going to be in trouble."

I had no idea what Abby's mom looked like, but she must have been beautiful. The only resemblance she had with her dad was the dark hair and naturally tan skin color. Other than that, they shared very little other features. Abby's eyes were an amazing emerald color, which I suspected she had inherited from her mother, along with the thick, vibrant red hair. I had never seen two more unique looking individuals in my life. He was going to have his hands full when she got older.

"Don't even get me started on the whole boy phase," Eric warned. "I'm half tempted to send her to a private all-girls school."

"Keep her involved in dog rescue." I told him without hesitating. Knowing firsthand how much time and energy went into saving dogs, there would be very little ambition left to spend chasing boys around.

"Do you want to add a child to your rescue?" He laughed, jokingly of course. "You seem to have a better idea how to raise them than I do!"

"I haven't the slightest clue how to raise a kid. I just wished I had found my passion for rescue a lot sooner than I had. Would have kept me out of a lot of trouble I imagine."

"I'm sure you were an angel growing up."

I was glad he didn't know anything about my past. I couldn't imagine him to think so highly of me had he known I spent most of my high school years partying and getting drunk.

"Hey," I changed the subject, "do you think it would be okay if I took Abby dress shopping for the event?"

"I didn't realize she was going to be invited, of course you can." Putting an arm around my waist he drew me closer and gave me a quick kiss while Abby was distracted with the dogs. "You really are amazing. I think she would love to have a girls day with you."

"It's going to be a 21 and older event, since there will be alcohol, but she is a part of the rescue. My event, my rules. Right?"

"I'm sure she would be flattered to hear she is a part of the rescue."

"Of course she is a part of it. You both are," I replied, snuggling deeper into his arm.

"When is this girls night out going to be?"

"Trish and I are going dress shopping next weekend. If you would like we could all meet up for dinner, then Abby can come with us and we'll drop her off on our way back."

"Sounds like a plan. I'll let you tell her though, I know she is going to be so excited."

He was right about that. I didn't think I'd ever seen someone more excited about anything in their life than Abby did when I asked her if she wanted to be a part of the big event. Her face glowed the rest of the evening as she pranced around the kennel helping out with chores.

All the event planning was almost finished, and Trish had already mailed out all the invitations as well as plastered it across social media. I was expecting a pretty good turn out as most of the guests we personally invited had already let us know they would be attending. Most of them were mutual friends of mine and Trish's from back in California, and money was no issue for them. Neither was hopping on a plane to attend an event clear across the country. As far as social media went, we already had over a hundred people click the 'attending' button on our facebook event page. Tickets weren't officially on sale yet, so I wasn't sure how many would actually go through with it.

"Have you heard back from your parents whether they're going to make it or not?" Eric asked as we followed Abby into my apartment to get Annie and my dogs out for some fresh air.

I handed Abby two leashes and asked if she could put them on Posh and Ace. "Yea, my dad called last night and told me he would for sure be here. Mom isn't sure if she will be able to make it though, with her work schedule and everything."

"What is it your parents do again?" he asked, probably wondering what was so important that her own mom couldn't attend an event her daughter was pouring her heart into.

"They both run a pretty big company and have crazy work schedules." That wasn't exactly the truth, but the fact that my dad owned the company was irrelevant. Truth was, they had always been more career focused than family. My mother especially.

"I was hoping they would both be able to make it. I feel like our last meeting didn't go so well."

"I wouldn't worry about it," I smiled. His intentions were sweet, but I was sure my mom would have something to say when she found out I was dating someone with a kid and I wanted to keep our relationship drama free for as long as possible. "I'm sure there will be another chance to meet her."

Watching Abby walk Posh, I smiled at the thought of how excited she was to be a part of the rescue. Posh had recently began to attach herself to the little girl and for once in the short time I'd had her, wanted nothing to do with me.

"I haven't seen her this happy in a long time," Eric said, as if he could read my mind. "I hope her coming around this much doesn't bother you."

"Absolutely not. I enjoy her being here." I didn't think I would take to his daughter as much as I had, but I really did enjoy having her around.

"Good. I think she would kill me if I left her behind, she loves this place so much."

For the first time in a few days, every single dog got out for a walk and by the end of the evening I was exhausted. It was the weekend and since Abby didn't have school in the morning, we decided to have a movie night. After fetching several dogs from their suites, we put on a dvd and everyone piled on and around the couch. If this was going to become a weekly event, I would have to re arrange my living room to accommodate everyone more comfortably.

"Daddy? Can I stay the night with Karen instead of going to grandmas tomorrow while you work?" Abby asked, looking at her dad and then me.

"That's up to Karen," he replied, "you know better than to put people on the spot like that though."

"It's fine by me," I piped in, trying to keep her from getting in trouble. "Trish will be here bright and early and she can help us pick up stuff for the party. I'll be a girls day until you get here."

Abby's face lit up. "Yes!"

Putting on his boots to head out, he asked one last time if I was sure it was okay. "I don't want us to become a bother?"

"Don't be silly," I smiled as we hugged each other good bye. "Drive safe and let me know when you make it home. We'll keep in touch tomorrow and let you know how the shopping goes."

"You be good for her, you hear?"

"Yes dad," Abby replied as she hugged and kissed him goodnight. "See you tomorrow. Love you."

Once Eric had gone, I made a bed for Abby on the couch and headed to my own. Looking around to see who was sleeping where, I noticed Posh making her way to the couch to sleep with her new best friend. "Traitor," I whispered happily.

Surprised I was awake before Trish showed up, I made a quick breakfast for the three of us before getting started on the chores. Throwing on a dozen extra eggs and scrambling them up, I emptied the pan into a large bowl once it had cooked. I felt more energized than I had in a while, despite the lack of sleep I had been getting, and decided to whip together an extra special breakfast for all the dogs. With my numbers now at fourteen dogs, it was hard to give them all special treatment, so a different breakfast would have to do.

Trish had just arrived as I finished making our food, and we were all sitting around the small kitchen table I had in my unfinished kitchen. Luckily, last week I stumbled upon a nice kitchen appliance set someone was selling for cheap to make room for their new set. Everything was kind of just thrown in there, and I still needed to find cabinets, but what I had worked for now.

"Is there anything I can do to help?" Abby asked once we had finished eating.

"Why don't you measure out the dogs food and get their bowls ready," I suggested. "You remember where the chart is with how much they all get, right?"

"Yes ma'am," she replied politely, taking the bowl of scrambled eggs I handed to her.

"Just split this up between all the bowls once you put their food in them. Trish and I will be there to help you pass them out once we finish cleaning the rooms out."

"She's really into this isn't she?" Trish asked once Abby had left. "I never thought I would say this, but you would make a great mom."

"Hey," I sneered. "None of that talk. I really like her, but nowhere in my near future will I be having one of my own."

"Well, like Eric said, she doesn't really have a mom since she basically walked out on them. So you are kind of taking on that role."

"I think of her more as a young friend, not a daughter," I corrected. "We are way too early in our relationship for me to start thinking I'm going to one day be her mom."

"I know. I'm just saying one day I think you will make a really good one. Whether it's to her, or your own."

"Right now let's just focus on the rescue," I laughed. "Speaking of which, we have kennels to clean."

"How are the new dogs doing?" Trish asked as we began gathering supplies.

"Rose and Lilly are doing really good, but only if they're kept together. The minute I take one away from the other they get really anxious. I'm afraid finding them a home together is going to be next to impossible so I don't know what I'm going to do there. Rocky, the little white terrier, is an angel. I can't believe no one snatched him up at the shelter."

"I'll have to get to work on the website so we can get them listed. Have you heard any more on the status of the nonprofit paperwork you filled out?"

"No, still waiting. I really hope it's all done in time for the event," I said as we disappeared into separate rooms to begin cleaning.

Abby came out and helped clean the last few rooms once she had finished preparing all the breakfasts. "I set them all in front of their rooms," she proudly informed us. "Do you want me to start pushing the bowls in to them?"

"Go ahead." I couldn't help but feel impressed with her determination to help as much as she could. For being so young, she really was a big help around here.

Having finished our event shopping earlier than planned, we decided to stop into a few dress stores that were on that side of town to get a head start on the impossible task of finding the perfect dress. Just as we were getting ready to leave, after each trying on half a dozen gowns, I spotted a dress behind the counter as we passed by.

"Is that one for sale?" I asked the sales associate who had been helping us out for the past hour.

Shaking her head, she told me it was but would probably be out of my price range. "It's a special vintage collection Madam Lura has just picked up. That dress came all the way from Paris last week and is the only one we have in stock.

Light pink in color, the dress was covered in sparkling diamonds and white lace elegantly trimmed the bottom. I had never seen a little girls dress look so astonishing, and was determined to get Abby in it.

"Can she try it on?" I asked politely, disregarding her rude comment about not being able to afford it.

"It would be a waste of time," the associate repeated. "The sale price on that particular dress, is over a thousand dollars."

"So, let me be the one to determine whether that is out of my price range or not." I was getting irritated with the way she was treating us and my patience was wearing thin. Slamming my purse down on the counter, I pulled out a credit card and handed it to her. "Spends just as well as cash, go ahead and run it, I assure you the money is there."

Taken back on my sudden change of attitude, the woman quickly snatched the dress off the rack and lead us back toward the fitting rooms. After knocking on a door to make sure it was unoccupied, she let Abby and myself in.

Helping her with all the buttons that ran up the back of the dress, I finally secured the last one and stood back to admire the piece of art. It had been a long time since I'd seen a dress of this quality, but with my history of apparel I was quick to recognize the value of such an outfit. Stepping out of the fitting room, I lead her to the stage surrounded by mirrors so she could see herself at all angles.

"Wow," Trish breathed. "That is stunning on her."

"I know, right! If only they had it in my size as well. How adorable would that be to have matching dresses for the ball."

I didn't have to ask what Abby thought of the dress, it was written all over her face. Turning around several times, watching as the lacey bottom flowed with every move, she looked up at me and smiled. "I've never wore anything like this before!"

The size was perfect, it couldn't have fit better if someone custom made it for her. Grabbing a pair of sparkling shoes off the display against the wall, I told her to try them on to see how they went with the dress.

"The outfit is perfect," I told Trish as we watched the little girl stare at herself in the reflection of the mirrors. "Every girl deserves to feel like a princess every now and again."

"What will it be then? Clearly it fits her, I hope you weren't wasting my time," the sales associate said as we returned to the check out.

This woman was getting on my last nerve. How dare she judge us just because we were in ratty work clothes and not some fancy designer piece. "I'll take it," I replied flashing her a snarky smile. "I'll also take a pair of the shoes she tried on, as well as that." I pointed at the tiara in the display case beneath her. "What's my total?"

"Three thousand two hundred. Will that be debit or credit."

Trish and Abby stood behind me, faces filled with horror as I turned back the woman and told her debit.

Once the dress was put into a garment bag, I scooped everything up and lead the way out of the store. Before walking out the door, I looked over my shoulder and smiled at the rude sales woman. "By the way, tell your boss I would like the same exact dress in a size 0. By next weekend."

Abby was quiet the entire ride home, staring out the window biting her lips nervously. Once we had pulled into her drive way, I asked her what was wrong.

"Ummm," she began shyly. "I don't think my dad has that kind of money to spend on a dress. I really like it, but I don't know how he is going to pay you back for it."

Laughing, I told her not to worry about it. "The price will be our little secret."

CHAPTER 8

Dogs continuously poured through our doors the entire week and by Friday there were almost a dozen on the euthanasia list. We had worked on setting up the intake room with the old kennels, but nothing could have prepared me for taking on this many dogs at once. Two of the dogs were so aggressive you couldn't get near them so despite wanting to save them all, I decided I simply didn't have the man power to take on such behavioral cases. It pained me having to leave them behind Friday after work knowing their fate, but I had to focus on the nine new dogs I just took in. I wasn't sure how I was going to take care everyone, but letting perfectly healthy animals die wasn't an option either. I could only hope that the gala next weekend would bring in a lot of money as well as adoptions. If anything it should at least spread the word about the rescue and send interest my way.

On a positive note, one of Trish's college acquaintances came by yesterday and adopted Rocky. It didn't free up much room, but for him it meant a shot at a good and happy life and that was all I could ask for. I had another girl interested in one of the two bonded pits, but I was really trying to get them a home together so I told her I'd let her know soon, hoping the gala would bring in someone looking for two perfectly behaved dogs. It was a shot in the dark, but I had to at least give them that chance at staying together.

Annie's progress was steadily increasing, she was finally acting like her old self and no longer had to sleep in the crate at night. Despite already having Ace, Posh and Reina staying in my apartment with me, she fit in so well with them that I couldn't bring myself to return her to her suite. Reina was supposed to go home with Eric and Abby the beginning of the week, but with them always over here it made more sense for her to just stay put. Instead, more often than not, Eric brought his dog Kato over when they came so he didn't have to stay home alone all the time. It didn't bother me none, the more dogs the better was my new motto.

I had anxiously been waiting for the phone call from the boutique we had gotten Abby's dress at, and finally this morning it came. They had my dress in, so we were headed there first before hitting up some other local shops to find one for Trish. I felt bad for spending that much money on dresses, with all the expenses coming up with the new dogs I was going to be tight until after the gala.

Before we walked in to make sure the dress was a good fit, Trish reminded me of my financial strain. "I understand the woman got under your skin last time, but try not to throw your money out to make a point."

"I know, I just didn't like the way she treated us. Just because we weren't in designer clothes carrying thousand dollar clutches, does not give her the right to treat us any differently," I pointed out as we were entering the store.

"Yea, well you and I both know that your personal collection you have back in California is probably worth double what they have in stock here," she whispered.

We both looked around, hoping it was a different sales associate there today and were disappointed to find the same rude woman staring smugly ahead at us.

"I'm here to try on my dress," I said flatly.

"I'll go ahead and grab it from the back and set you up in the first fitting room," she smiled, forcing herself to be nice.

I wondered if the phone call I had made earlier that week to the store owner got her in any trouble. She hadn't seemed too pleased to hear that her associate had been rude to us, and told me she would take care of the matter. Obviously, customer service wasn't a top priority since the woman was still employed here.

Rolling my eyes as I watched her disappear into the back, I saw Trish shoot me a warning look. It wasn't my intention to start any drama today. I just wanted to get my dress and get out. I would find the rest of my accessories at another store.

The fit was perfect, so with no need to set up an alteration appointment, I quickly paid and bolted for the door before my mouth said something it shouldn't.

"I'm proud of you," Trish said as she threw her arm over my shoulder. "The old you would have put that woman through the ringer, but you controlled yourself very well in there."

"I don't have the energy to pick a fight right now. With everything going on and the gala less than a week away, I'm wore right out."

"She wasn't worth it anyway. Did you see her shoes? They were not designer quality by any means. She's probably hates her job, watching everyone come in and buy the things she wishes she could."

"You have a point," I laughed. "You remember saying how my collection was probably worth more than what they had in stock? Well it gave me a really good idea. How many of our friends always commented on how they would die for my collection? Since most of the people attending the gala are going to be wealthy socialites, what if I had my dad pack up all my stuff and bring it out. We could auction it all off to raise more money for the rescue. Can you imagine how much that would bring in."

"You love your collection though. I can't believe you would actually sell it all."

"When am I ever going to have the time to wear any of that stuff now? I certainly am not going to clean the kennels or walk dogs in my $2000 pair of Christian Louboutin heals. Besides, I don't really think Eric is the type to care if I wear designer clothes or something from a thrift shop."

"Wait…" Trish laughed. "Did I just hear the word thrift shop, come out of Karen VanOlsen's mouth?"

"Yes, actually you did. The other day I stopped by one while I was up town picking up more dog food. Just out of curiosity you know, and they actually had some really nice stuff in there. I even bought a few pairs of jeans, and a really cute top for Abby."

"I think I've heard it all now."

"Don't laugh, I'm running out of money and all my clothes are destroyed. I needed something cheap and didn't feel like shopping around for a bargain."

"I'm not laughing at you, I just think it's ironic. You always used to tease that poor sophomore, what was her name?"

"Tammy." I couldn't believe how mean I was to her, it made me feel bad having it brought up.

"Yea, Tammy. You caught her coming out of the thrift store one time and never let her live it down."

"I can't believe how shallow and mean I used to be. It kind of makes me sick to my stomach looking back at it all now."

"Well, you're different now and that's all that matters."

It didn't take long for Trish to pick out a dress, she was about the least picky person I knew when it came to fashion. The dress was stunning on her, however. I always told her red was her color, it just went so well with her porcelain complexion. When she actually took the time to do her hair and makeup, she was by far one of the prettiest girls I'd ever seen, not that she wasn't drop dead gorgeous without any. Very few people could pull off a natural look, and she was lucky enough to be among them.

"I still can't believe how much I spent on mine and Abby's dresses when yours only cost a fraction of the price and looks just as good. I guess that's how the designer world goes though, you pay for the name. Hopefully my idea for the auction goes over well."

"I'm sure it will. I know for a fact that Britany has been lusting after that cheetah print Louis Vuitton bag your parents got you for your twentieth birthday. Didn't that come right off the runway?"

"Yea, and it cost over five grand," I pointed out. Mentally running through everything I had, I figured I must have over a hundred thousand worth between shoes, bags and clothes. One pair of heels in particular were worth ten grand alone.

"Are you sure your parents will let you have your stuff? Wasn't that one of the stipulations, that you had to leave with nothing?"

"I think if I talk to my dad, and explain what I wanted it for, he would totally go for it. I'll leave mom out of it though. She would probably kill me if she found out I was auctioning off everything she spent her money on. You know how she is."

"We'll find out for sure tonight, and I'll send a group message out to everyone on the rsvp list and let them know about the auction. Speaking of which, have you checked the ticket sales yet this morning?"

"No," I replied, as we pulled up to the warehouse. Abby had realized last minute that her schools end of year field trip was today, and wasn't able to make it out for our girls day. I was pretty sure she would have traded the day at the amusement park to hang out with us. I actually felt myself missing her throughout the day and was glad when Eric text me saying they would be over tonight.

"I checked last night, and we're up to 390 people attending that have already purchased their tickets, and there's over a hundred more that have shown interest but haven't paid yet. I think were actually going to sell out."

"I can't believe this is actually happening. Between the tickets and auction, we should have no problem remodeling this entire warehouse. It would be nice to get a whole new facility outside of the city, but there's no way we will raise enough to make that happen. That will have to come after I get my inheritance, which hopefully my dad can convince my mom to let me have sooner than later."

"No kidding," Trish scowled. "They have to see how much you've changed and how far you have come since moving here. I mean, I'm your best friend and I still find myself in shock every day at how different you are. I honestly thought we were going to drift apart after I moved out here for school, and you stayed back in California. I remember begging you to move out here with me and all you cared about was partying and what not."

I still couldn't believe what kind of person I used to be. I didn't care about anyone other than myself. It was actually rather embarrassing, and I wondered how many other people felt that way about me. "Eric and Abby will be here shortly, do you want to stay for movie night?" I asked, changing the subject. "I'm ordering pizza….with pineapple."

"Well in that case, heck yeah! You know I can't refuse pizza and pineapple!"

After getting all the dogs out for their walk, which didn't take long when there was four of us, we settled in and ordered dinner. I would eventually have to hire someone to help with all the dogs, unfortunately that would have to wait until the funds began coming in, until then I would just have to push through and do as much as I could. It was a lot of help when everyone came and pitched in, which happened more than not, so I was grateful for that. The hardest part was getting everyone out for exercise, so I started thinking of ways to get it done without having to pay someone a full time wage. I decided to run my idea past everyone and now that we were all sitting around the table together, I proposed my plan.

"So I have been thinking." Taking a drink of soda to wash down my last bite of pizza, I looked around to make sure I had everyone's attention. "What if we advertised some kind of a program where people who wanted to lose weight, or just get out and exercise, met up here every night at a certain time and we all did a group walk together. It would not only help get the dogs out, but it would socialize them and get them used to new people as well. Do you think we would get much interest in something like that?"

"Even if we got a few people, it would be better than none," Trish pointed out. "We could definitely start advertising that we need volunteers on the new site now that it's finally up and running."

"I think that would be a great idea. I think a lot of people want to exercise but lose motivation after a while. This would be a great way to keep them focused," Eric pitched in.

"Alright then, Trish, do you want to post something online this evening and see what kind of feedback we get?"

"I'm on it," she laughed. Phone already in her hand, she began punching away at the keyboard.

"While she is busy doing that, who wants to help me round up some of the dogs for movie time?" I winked at Abby, knowing that was what she had been waiting for all night.

"Who's all coming in tonight?" she asked excitedly as she jumped up and headed for the door.

Looking at the five dogs that lay passed out around the room, I thought of who best got along with everyone. "Why don't you grab Mia and I'll get Star."

"I'll clean up dinner so we don't have any fights over the pizza on the table," Eric said as he began piling the plates on top of each other to throw out.

"That's probably a good idea." I winked at him as Abby lead the way out to get the dogs. It had been awhile since we shared any alone time, and I was desperately craving a kiss from him. We tried not to show too much affection toward one another in front of his daughter, but with her always being around it was getting harder and harder.

"So I heard Abby found a dress when you guys went out for supplies last weekend. What do I owe you?" Eric pulled out his wallet, probably expecting to be able to pay for it in cash.

"Don't worry about it," I smiled. "It's already taken care of."

"Don't be silly. I can't let you do that, it was probably expensive."

Expensive was a little bit of an understatement. "No, it was on sale for a good price. It's my gift, I already told her that."

"Well, thank you. Just know that I don't expect you to buy her stuff, and she doesn't either." Sliding closer as the movie began, he put his arm around my shoulder and smiled.

It felt nice being in his arms again. Abby was more occupied with the dogs than the movie, and I was pretty sure we didn't even exist at that point. Resting my head on his shoulder, I felt him lean down and kiss my forehead. Butterflies danced around my stomach, as they did every time he kissed me.

Just as we had all gotten settled in and relaxed, all of a sudden an eruption of barking and growling broke out behind us. Jumping up, I tripped over two dogs laying at my feet and came crashing down onto a third. Before I could get up, I heard Abby scream and saw Eric go over the back of the couch to get to her. By the time I got to them, I realized Abby was in the middle of a fight between Reina and Annie.

"That's enough!" I yelled, grabbing the closest dog to me by her back legs. When that didn't break up the fight I ran to the shelf where

I always kept an airhorn in case something like this were to happen. The noise that it made when I pushed the handle down was enough to make everyone in the room go deaf, and luckily it distracted the two dogs enough for me to get them away from each other.

Putting Annie back in her crate after quickly looking her over, I asked Trish to check Reina out while I went to make sure Abby was okay. "What happened?" I asked, once everything had calmed down.

"I was playing with them with the tug rope I grabbed from Reina's kennel when I brought her in here," she told me. I was surprised at how calm she was for just being in the middle of a dog fight.

It was my fault for not telling her that Annie wasn't allowed to be around other dogs when there were toys out. "I should have told you this earlier, but Annie resource guards."

"What does that mean?" she asked, looking like she was about to cry. "Is it my fault they got into a fight."

"No, absolutely not. It's my fault for not telling you. Resource guarding means a dog will be possessive over an item, like a toy or a bone or their food. Anything they feel is theirs, they will sometimes fight another dog for if they get too close or try to take it."

"I should have asked you if I could play with them," she said as a tear rolled down her cheek. "I'm really sorry."

"You had no way of knowing." I wrapped my arms around her and felt her start crying more. "Sometimes dogs get into fights, it's just how it goes. Luckily no one got hurt, so there's nothing to worry about sweetie."

"Are you sure you're not mad at me?"

"Positive!" I looked down at her and smiled. "Now why don't you bring Reina over to the couch and cuddle up with the rest of us."

"What about Annie?" she asked, clearly feeling bad for the dog.

"Annie needs some time alone right now, to calm down. She'll be okay in her crate for a while."

The remainder of the night went without any more incidents, and by the time everyone left I was ready to call it a night. Tomorrow started the first official day of set up for the event, and with how much still needed to be done, I couldn't afford to be sluggish.

I had less than a week left to get everything done, and that included getting the dogs comfortable crossing over the stage. It didn't seem like a big deal, but I wanted to make sure they walked nicely across it as well as show off a few of the commands they knew. Anything to help them get adopted. I also wanted to decorate the kennel and make it look extra nice for when we did tours to show everyone the facility. The list of what needed to get done was never ending.

I was only scheduled to work a few days that week, which would help free up my time immensely, but I still needed as much help as I could get so I shot Trish a quick text asking if she made it home alright, followed by a desperate plea to ask Ashley and her boyfriend to come over and help whenever they got the chance. Then I made a quick phone call to my dad to talk to him about packing up my wardrobe and bringing it down for me to auction off.

By the time I finally got to crawl into bed, I no more than got comfortable when Ace started whining. As much as I wanted to ignore him, I shot him an annoyed glance and asked if he had to go out, which of course sent all three dogs into a frenzy. I really needed to get a fenced in yard with a doggie door installed.

CHAPTER 9

It was halfway through the week and the event room was already looking spectacular. It amazed me how quickly something could be put together when professional crews came in to do the work instead of a bunch of novices. With that side of things basically taken care of, I focused all my time on working with the dogs to get them show ready. Every day I spent time with each dog, working on their basic obedience commands as well as walking on a loose leash. The few that were still uneasy around new people, I took to the park to work on their social skills. For someone who didn't know much about training, I felt rather proud for how well everyone was doing. Even Jaxx did surprisingly well when Trish and I took him to the park, not that he was anywhere near being ready for adoption. I didn't want to leave him out however. I had a sad feeling he would be living the rest of his life out here at the rescue, so I tried to spoil him whenever I could. Every time I looked at him, I could feel myself begin to fill with rage at what those idiots did to make him this way. I was also reminded of all the dogs that sat waiting for the court to decide what would happen with them. Last I had heard they were still on hold, and that had been over a week ago. Elaine was probably getting tired of calling all the time to check their status, but she did it for me anyway.

It was almost noon, and I had already gotten through a lot of the training so I decided to take a quick break and pick Abby up from school since she only had a half day. Eric had mentioned a few evenings ago that she only had a few days left before summer break, and with the last two of them being half days, he would either have to take time off of work or find a sitter since his mom was out of town for the week. Without hesitating, I volunteered to be at his house when she got off the bus and bring her back to the warehouse until he was off duty. I was getting burned out from working with the dogs so much, and had a feeling they could sense my frustration since most of the morning I spent fighting with them over things they already knew, so I decided to skip waiting around and pick her directly up from school.

Trish was pulling a late shift at the vet clinic, so since she wouldn't be able to make it over, I decided to give her a quick call while waiting for Abby to come out.

"I have good news," she immediately said upon answering the phone.

"I could use some of that right now," I laughed, excited to hear what she had to say.

"I forgot to check the ticket sales yesterday, and this morning when I looked, you won't believe how many we have sold since posting about the auction."

"I'm listening," I said excitedly when she paused for suspense.

"Were up to five hundred that are paid for, and there have been several people comment asking for pictures of some of the attire. Not to mention the text I got this morning from our dear friend Britany asking if you were going to be auctioning that Louis Vuitton bag. When I told her yes, she demanded that as her friend, you just sell it to her outright instead of making her get into a bidding war over it."

"I don't even know what to say! I hope everything goes as planned and we don't let all these people down," I replied nervously. Never had I imagined it would get this big, and now that it was I didn't know if I was prepared enough. "Did she give you a price she would pay for it?"

"She said you name the price and she'd pay it."

"Did you give her a price," I asked, knowing where this was going.

"I told her that you were going to start the bid off at five thousand, and that I was sure it would go much higher once the bidding started, so we would take ten for it."

"You sold her the bag for ten thousand dollars?" I shrieked. The woman in the car next to me nearly jumped out of her seat then gave me a dirty look, understandably embarrassed. "Did she actually say she would pay it?"

"She's already sent the money. I told her she could pick it up when she got here this weekend."

"Unbelievable." Abby was headed toward the bus so I told Trish I would call her later as I jumped out and ran after her before she got on. "Abby!"

Turning to see who was calling her name, she smiled when she saw me. "I thought you were picking me up at my house?"

"I didn't see any point in making you ride the bus, besides I needed a break from working with the dogs. Do you need anything from home?"

"Nope." She happily followed me back to the car and slid into the passenger seat after putting her bookbag in the back. "So who is left to work with?"

"Well, I want to do some more leash work with the bonded pair, and Star still needs some work on her stay. Other than that, I got almost everyone done already this morning. If we have time we can do some more work with the new dogs since they're pretty restless and could use an energy release."

"It'll be nice once the outdoor yard gets put up," she pointed out. "I can't wait to watch them be able to run around and play."

"That makes two of us," I laughed. "Do you have any homework you need to get done before we get started when we get back?"

"We never have homework the last few days of school. I don't even know why they bother making us come in."

It hadn't been that long ago since I was goofing off in school, but seeing how I never attended the last few days, I wouldn't know what went on. I couldn't believe I even passed my senior year with how much school I skipped.

"You grab Rose and I'll meet you out front with Lilly," I told her once we pulled up to the warehouse. For being only eleven, Abby was really good at working with the dogs, like she had been doing it her whole life. She had more patience than I did, which went a long way with training dogs.

Rose was the much calmer of the two, so it didn't take much for Abby to get her to pay attention to her. Lilly on the other hand, was all over the place this afternoon. It took a half hour for me to get her to start paying attention to me, and by that time my patience was wearing thin.

"Want to switch dogs?" Abby asked, seeing me struggle to keep my composure as the pit bull wandered back and forth pulling on the leash.

"Are you sure you can handle her?"

Abby laughed as she pointed out that I wasn't really a whole lot bigger than her. "Here, take Rose."

Exchanging dogs, I watched her work her magic and within ten minutes the carefree dog had her full attention on the little girl. I didn't know how she did it.

Ending the training session with a quick walk around the block, I was excited to see both dogs walking nicely at our sides. The next thing we would eventually have to work on was separating them from each other. That would be a lesson for another day since I still had hope that they would find their forever home together.

Once I had Star out in the parking lot, I asked her for a sit, which she did immediately, then I gave the 'stay' command and slowly backed up a few steps. I could tell she was about to get up and follow me, so I quickly told her good girl as I walked back and offered a treat. We did this several times, each time adding another step or two in between us. By the end of the session, I was able to get about ten feet away before she started to get anxious and wanted to join me. Deciding to end on a good note, I did a quick refresher on some of the commands she was more familiar with then lead her back to her room where I emptied my pocket of the rest of the treats.

"Can we get Alex out next?" Abby asked.

Alex was one of the new dogs I had recently rescued from the shelter, and he came with an endless supply of bad habits. His main one was leash biting, which wouldn't have been that big a deal had he not already bit my hand as he worked his way up the leash. He was a sweet dog, so I really wanted to get him adoptable before the event, but with it being only a few days away I didn't see that happening. I wouldn't necessarily deny him a home if the right person came along, but they would have to agree to get him the training he needed to prevent his problems from worsening.

I started off by walking into his room with the leash behind my back, only after he gave me a sit when I asked did I present him with the leash. Immediately he jumped up and began trying to bite it, which I figured it was out of excitement. Taking the leash back out of his sight I made him sit again before showing it to him once he calmed down. After several attempts, he finally stayed in a sitting position so I immediately rewarded him with a treat and attached the leash to his collar. As we walked out of the room, he started his leash biting and worked his way up until I only had a few inches left before it was my hand. Quickly, I took my leg and bumped him in the hind end and told him no. Looking up at me confused, I rewarded him again by giving him a treat for taking his focus off the leash and putting it on me. We did this all the way until we were out of the kennel. It seemed like he relaxed a bit once we were outside away from the rest of the dogs, so I began working on his walking skills. It was possible that his behavior had something to do with stress from the kennel environment, since he only did it when other dogs where around. Either way, I would continue to work on it until he was adopted, which hopefully happened before he acquired any other undesirable behaviors.

It was just starting to get dark when Eric finally pulled up right in the middle of feeding time. Without asking, he jumped in and began helping.

"How was your day?" he asked once we finally finished and had time to catch up. "Was Abby good for you?"

"Of course she was, when is she not?" I opened the doors to the event room to show him all the progress that had been made today. "We've had quite a full day. Abby was a lot of help with the dogs, which caused me to think of something I want to run by you."

"Okay, let's hear it."

"Well, once this event is done, I really want to take a training course so we can better work with the problem dogs, and I want Abby to take it with me. I could hire her to help during the summer so she can start learning more and make some money. Only if that's alright with you though." I really hoped he'd agree, she had a gift and I wanted to see her reach her full potential. I also wanted to keep her busy so she didn't go down the same path I had.

"I know she would absolutely love that, but isn't she a little young to be taking classes like that?"

"I don't think so," I replied hesitantly. I didn't want to step on any feet when it came to parenting, but I also didn't want him to dismiss it as an option. "Age wise, yes she might be a little young, but she has a gift. You should see her working with the dogs. She can do things that I couldn't if I tried. I think it's worth some thought, and I would pay for all the class fees of course."

"I'll think about it. I just don't want to rush her childhood," he said as he took my hand. "I really do appreciate all the effort you're putting into being a part of her life though. She really looks up to you."

"It's no effort at all," I smiled. "I really enjoy her being around and helping out."

As we walked through the room, I pointed out what still needed to be done and tried to give him a mental picture of what it would look like when finished. When I told him how much we had made in sales already, his jaw about hit the floor.

"That's incredible! I'm really happy this is all coming together for you. I know how much work you've put into making this a success."

I left out the fact that the ticket sales would be nothing compared to how much the auction would bring in. I knew eventually I would have to tell him about my past, I just wasn't sure how to bring it up or when the appropriate time would be. I didn't want him to think any differently about me, so I just kept it to myself.

"So do I need to get a tux for this event?" he laughed. "It seems to be quite the ordeal and I don't want to show up under dressed."

"I think you would look really handsome in one," I hinted. "I mean you could show up in your police uniform and you would still look amazing."

"I think we will go with a tux."

"Good choice!" I loved seeing him in uniform, but imagining what he would look like dressed up had my heart beating a little faster.

"Am I going to get to see you in your dress beforehand or do I have to wait until that night?"

"You have to wait." I wanted mine and Abby's matching dresses to be a surprise or I would have already shown him by now. "Speaking of which, can you have Abby here around noon? I have salon appointments set up for us all to get our hair done."

"Not a problem."

The following two days went by so fast, it was a miracle we got everything done by Friday night. I didn't want to be working on any last minute details the day of the event, so I pushed for everyone that was available to meet up on Thursday and tie up all the loose ends. With the event less than a day away, all that was left to do was wait, and work with the dogs.

Eric and Trish showed up that evening, Abby had been with me all day, so the four of us each grabbed a dog and started working on simple basic commands as a last time refresher before their big debut. I hoped with all the work we had put into their training the past week, they would all be on their best behavior and win over the hearts of everyone who showed up.

I made a mental note of who connected with which dogs, so I could best pair them up during the event. Abby would definitely be in charge of Rose, since she didn't pay much attention to anyone else who tried working with her. I also planned to have her show Tucker, the little brown pit mix who came in last week as well as Star.

"You're doing a great job!" I yelled across the event room as I watched Abby work with Rose on her fear of the stages steps. Looking around, I saw Eric at work making Pearl sit and lay down in the middle of the stage while he stood next to her for few moments. I had made up little index cards with information on each of the dogs we would be taking, and as we crossed the stage we would stop in the middle and make the dog sit while we read their short bio.

Almost all of the dogs had run through the steps at least twice, some of them three times, and as far as I was concerned not one of them did a bad job. I still had one dog of my own to work with, but I would have to wait until the rest were put back in their rooms before bringing him out. Jaxx was by no means up for adoption, but I still wanted his story to be heard and for him to get the chance to meet new people. I planned on introducing a program where people could sponsor a dog that wasn't adoptable, and figured he would make the perfect candidate. After his short bio was read, I would introduce the program which people could sign up for that night if they so desired. Every table was going to have pamphlets on the rescue, as well as envelopes for donations and sponsorship information.

Standing outside of Jaxx's room, I could tell something wasn't right. He wasn't bouncing off the walls, or jumping at the gate excited for his turn to come. Instead, I found him curled up in the corner, snuggled into his blanket. Even as I walked into his room, he barely lifted his head to acknowledge me.

"What's the matter buddy?" I whispered sweetly, expecting him to jump up when he caught sight of the leash. When even that didn't happen, I called for Trish to come over and take a look at him.

"His gums are a good color and he isn't showing any signs of dehydration, his breathing is a little funny though. Let me grab my bag and I'll have a listen to his heart and lungs.

Before she returned, Abby came over to see what the hold up was, and I could tell she was on the verge of tears when I told her something was wrong with him. "I'm sure he will be fine," I lied, trying to reassure her. Truth was, I had never seen him act like this and it had me a little worried.

Just as Trish was putting her stethoscope away, Jaxx started coughing. It was the first time I'd ever heard him cough and I quickly looked up at Trish expecting her to know what to do.

"I hate to say this," she began, "but I think you should take him to the vet first thing in the morning to have him tested for heartworm."

That wasn't ideal with it being the day of the event, but nothing was more important than the health of my dogs so I quickly agreed with her.

"I know you have a lot going on tomorrow, so if you want I can take him to my clinic bright and early and run some tests. Depending on the results, it might be best if he just stay there." She looked down at me apologetically, knowing this was the last thing I needed to add to my already full plate.

"I'd appreciate that."

Forgetting that Eric and Abby were both standing outside of the room watching us, when I got up to leave I saw Abby burry her face into her dads waist and start crying.

"He's going to be alright." Trish told her, "a lot of dogs come in with heartworm and we get them all fixed up in no time."

"How did he get it?" she asked, wiping her eyes.

"It's passed to a dog when they come into contact with a mosquito that is carrying the parasite. It's fairly common around here, and as long as we caught it early enough, Jaxx should have no problem recovering with treatment."

I could tell Abby was still upset, so instead of sitting around the rest of the evening thinking about it, I suggested we take a few dogs down for some ice cream to get our minds on something else.

CHAPTER 10

Trish had just left for the clinic with Jaxx when I heard a knock on the entrance door. Looking over at Eric and Abby, their curiosity mirrored mine as to who could be showing up at this time of the morning. Opening the door, I took a step back in shock as I saw my dad standing there holding a huge bouquet of flowers in his hand. Quickly taking them, I set them on the closest table and threw my arms around him in a hug.

"I'm so proud of you Honeybee." Hearing him call me the nickname he had given me when I was little sent goosebumps down my arms. It had been years since he had called me that. I actually got the name when I used to make him come play tea party with me out on the back terrace under a lilac tree. The sweet smell of the flowers always attracted the honey bees over to join in on our tea time. It was my favorite place as a little girl, and that's when he started calling me that.

"You're early!" I said excitedly. "I thought your flight wasn't supposed to arrive until noon and I was picking you up?"

"Did you really think I would be able to bring all your clothes in carry on bags and suitcases? Besides, I have another surprise for you."

"First, let me introduce you to someone," I smiled as I motioned for Abby and Eric to come over.

"You've already briefly met Eric, and this is his daughter Abby," I said proudly. I never had to worry about my dad being judgmental so it was with a lot of pride that I introduced my boyfriend and his child.

"Nice to meet you, again." Shaking Erics hand, he then turned his attention to Abby. "And it's certainly a pleasure to meet you. Have you been keeping my little girl out of trouble?"

Laughing at my dad calling me his little girl, she politely told him yes sir.

Glad that everyone had met, I let my dad lead the way outside to reveal his big surprise. "This is the main reason why I drove instead of taking the flight," he smiled as my car came into view. "Your mother agreed to let you have it back."

My jaw hit the floor when I saw my shiny, custom painted, red Cadillac sitting in the parking lot. "No way," I stammered in disbelief. "She actually said I can have it?"

"She's more proud of you than you realize. You know how she is, showing emotion isn't her strong suit. That doesn't mean she doesn't feel it though."

"This is great!" I shrieked, hugging my dad once again. Suddenly remembering that Eric had no idea of my former life, I quickly asked if he could give it to me as a gift instead of saying it was already mine.

My dad was no dummy though and quickly caught on. "He has no idea who you really are, does he?"

"I didn't know how to tell him. I mean what do I say when meeting someone? Hey my names Karen and I'm pretty much a millionaire? How would I ever meet a guy that actually wants me and not just my money or status?"

"None of that used to matter to you. Flaunting your money used to be your favorite past time."

"Well it isn't anymore," I snapped. Realizing I was being rude, I quickly apologized and told him that wasn't who I was anymore.

"Clearly." Looking me up and down, then over toward the warehouse, he smiled. "I like the woman you have turned into way better. I'll go along with your little lie, but you have to promise to tell him soon. He is going to figure somethings up when you start dragging in thousands of dollars' worth of shoes."

Laughing, I reminded him that Eric was a cop, and probably wouldn't have the first clue as to who Giorgio Armani or any other of the designers were. "I do promise to tell him though."

"Good. Now let's get this car unloaded, I promised your mother I would pick her up from the airport when the flight I was supposed to be on landed."

"Wait," I said suddenly stopping in my tracks. "Moms coming?

"I couldn't let a nonrefundable ticket go to waste," he winked. "She told me to tell you that she has a surprise."

"What kind of surprise?" I asked, afraid of the answer.

"I honestly have no idea, she wouldn't tell me. You know I can't keep secrets."

This was probably not going to be good.

"So I have good news and bad news," Trish announced as she walked through the salon doors to meet up with Abby and I. "Bad news is, Jaxx's bloodwork showed up positive for heartworm."

"Good news is that its early stage right?" I asked hopefully.

"Yes, it's not too far along for treatment, and he should be back to his grumpy old self in no time. The vet said he sees no reason to keep him out of the event, and that if anything it might help raise awareness to keep the audiences dogs protected from getting infected. He did say to keep it short and sweet, however, and not put him through too much since he is a little under the weather.

"Is he acting more lively than he was last night? I don't want to cause him anymore stress than I have to."

"He's still acting a little tired, but after eating two cans of dog food he perked up a little. Why don't we wait and see how he is feeling this evening and decide then."

"Sounds like a good idea." I was glad to hear that he would be okay, but the idea of putting him into any kind of stressful situation didn't sit too well. If he was acting fine this evening, we would go ahead as planned, but if not than his story would be told without him present.

Sitting down in front of the mirror, I looked at my reflection and cringed. It just now hit me how much I had let myself go as I noticed the shape my hair was in, which was nothing compared to the dark circles under my eyes.

"I hope you're in the business of performing miracles," I told the stylist as she walked over and introduced herself.

"I'll have you looking brand new in no time," she laughed. "Lets start with these roots. When was the last time you had them done?"

"It's been a while," I admitted embarrassedly.

"I see that. I suggest we add a few lowlights into your blonde since you are probably going to have a bleach line from letting it grow out so long. Is that alright with you?"

"Whatever you think will look best." I apparently wasn't going to have the time anymore to keep up with platinum blonde hair, so maybe adding some dark to it would help me in between touch ups.

Since my hair had to process and then be blown out before they could even start on the style, I told Trish to take Abby next door once their updo's were done and get started on their manicures.

Two hours passed before my stylist was finally able to start pinning my hair into a sleek and elegant bun at the base of my neck. Leaving a few strands of perfectly curled hair loose around my face,

I admired the masterpiece she had created and remembering what it looked like when I first sat down

After leaving my stylist a very nice tip to show my appreciation, I joined the girls next door to get my own nails done. I had originally planned on getting fake ones put on, but after looking at the clock I decided to just have them throw on a quick coat of pink polish as we still had to pick Jaxx up and get then dressed.

The event was due to start in less than half an hour by the time we arrived back at the warehouse, so after getting Jaxx settled back into his room, I helped Abby into her dress and then threw my own on. Having forgotten to take the tiara I had bought for Abby to the salon, I carefully placed it among her curls and stood back and smiled.

"You look stunning."

Trish sprayed both of our hair one last time and then handed me the hair spray so I could do hers before we headed out to meet up with Eric and my parents.

Putting my arm around Abby as we walked through the door, I couldn't help but smile when I saw Eric's reaction. Trish must of noticed it as well and leaned over to whisper in my ear that she had never seen a man smile the way he was right now.

"Wow." He twirled me around and then his daughter, admiring us both in different ways. "There are no words."

"Isn't it cool that we match!" Abby blurted out after giving her dad a hug.

"It is really cool." Looking over at me he smiled and gave a subtle wink. "I also have a surprise for the both of you."

Digging in his jacket pocket, I watched as he pulled out a little box and handed it to his daughter. Inside was a beautiful corsage with two small white flowers surrounding a bigger bright pink one. Purple ribbon weaved its way through the flowers and came to an elegant tail at the end and draped perfectly down Abby's wrist after Eric helped her put it on.

"And for you." He pulled out a much smaller box, one that couldn't possibly be holding a corsage. Handing it to me he must had seen the horrified expression on my face and quickly reassured me that it wasn't an engagement ring.

Letting out a deep breath, I continued to carefully open the jewelry box. Sitting inside was a beautiful pink diamond ring with white diamonds surrounding it in double layers and then continuing onto the band. Taking my hand, he gently slid it onto my finger and then kissed me, in front of everyone.

"I don't know what to say." I whispered, still in shock of the rings beauty.

"You don't have to say anything, I told you it wasn't an engagement ring. I just wanted to get you something that says how much I appreciate you."

"Thank you." Reaching up to give him another kiss, I looped my arms around his neck and stayed that way until we were interrupted by the person in charge of the guest list and ticket sales.

"Excuse me," he began uncomfortably as he realized he had just stumbled into the middle of a romantic moment. "The guests are arriving."

Jumping into motion, I cued for the band to begin playing softly as we had discussed when I hired them, and then made my way to where the caterers were standing in a group talking and told them they could begin making their way around with trays of hors d'oeuvres and drinks.

I had originally planned on holding a live auction, but after seeing how much attire my dad had arrived with, I decided on a silent auction instead. Earlier that week, Trish and I had gone around to local businesses and asked if anyone could donate their products or services to put up for auction. We had received quite a few baskets as well as gift certificates which we placed on a table next to where the rest of the auction items were being held.

Watching as people began pouring into the room, I realized that I still hadn't seen my parents. My father had mentioned picking my mom up from the airport this afternoon, but I hadn't heard anything since we last spoke before he left.

Sneaking out of the room, I pulled up his number and was sent right to voice mail. "Whatever," I mumbled to myself as I made my way back to where Eric and Abby were standing.

"That's a lot of people," Abby pointed out.

Scanning the room one more time, I told them I would be right back as I spotted a group of girls from my school. Catching Trish's eye, I motioned for her to join me.

"Britany, Tonya, Sarah! How have you guys been?" I asked politely when we finally reached them and hugs had been exchanged.

"I can't believe you left California to come out here and open an animal shelter," Sarah whispered, thinking the other girls couldn't hear her. "You had such a good life back then."

Trying not to be rude to my guests, I simply replied, "And I have an even better life now." I knew how each and every one of these girls worked, after all they had been my best friends all the way up until the day I had to leave. "Why don't you all get a drink and go take a look at what's up for auction, I'll catch up with you soon!"

Sneaking back to Eric's side, I sighed in relief at having that little reunion over with, that is until I saw who walked through the door next. Following behind my dad, was my mother, strolling proudly in all her elegance with a guy half her age attached to her arm. However, it wasn't my flashy mother that caused the air to get trapped in my lungs, it was who she had on her arm. In that moment I wanted to disappear. Quickly looking for an escape route, my mom caught sight of me before I could bolt off into any direction other than theirs.

"Karen!" she cackled from across the room, waving her hand at me.

"Is that your mom?" Abby asked, putting her arm around my waist and drawing herself closer to me. I had sent Eric off to get us a drink as soon as I caught sight of my parents, and hoped he got lost and took a while to return.

"Unfortunately," I whispered.

"Why isn't she holding your dads hand? Who is that guy that's with her?"

"That is a good question, one however that I have no answer for." Watching them draw closer, I felt myself begin to sweat and dabbed my face with the back of my hand.

"Karen," my mom said again, as she approached and gave me a quick hug. "You look a lot better than the last time we saw you."

"Yea, thanks mom. Um, why is Brody here, on your arm, at my event?"

"Why he is my guest. I thought you would be pleased to see him again. It's been what, 3 years since the two of you have had a chance to catch up?"

"That's because you don't normally 'catch up' with ex boyfriends," I mumbled under my breath.

I wasn't sure if she heard me since she was suddenly focused on something else. "Why is there a little girl dressed exactly like you at adult only event?"

"This is Abby, Eric's daughter." Knowing it wouldn't get left at that, I added, "you remember, the police officer that you kicked out of my hospital room?"

"Of course I remember. That doesn't explain why she is here in a ball gown dressed just like you."

Looking from my dad, back to my mom and then over to my ex boyfriend, I announced that Eric and I had been seeing each other just as I caught sight of him making his way through the crowd with our drinks.

"Here you are dear," he handed me my glass and then gave Abby hers. Unaware of the tension built up around him, he smiled at my dad and said it was nice to see him again and then extended a hand toward my mom. "Ma'am, I hope you had a good flight."

My mother stood there for a moment before politely shaking his hand and then turning her attention back to me. "You're dating a cop? A cop. Really Karen?"

"Yes mother, really. If you have a problem with that than why don't you just leave," I replied boldly. "And you dad, how could you let her do this!"

"Wait a minute," Eric began, "I feel like I'm missing something."

"A couple zeros at the end of your paycheck," Brody sneered.

"Excuse me? Who are you again?" Eric asked confused.

"Karen's ex, I'm sure she's mentioned me."

"Actually, no. I've never heard of you before. My question is, why are you here?"

Shooting me a confident look, Brody laughed. "Isn't it obvious? I'm here to take Karen back."

Looking at the guy I had once thought to be the most gorgeous guy around, I suddenly felt nothing but anger and resentment towards him. "I'm not going anywhere with you!"

"Karen! Don't talk to him like that, you're not thinking rationally right now," scorned my mother. "Brody has just flown across the country to come see you, the least you could do is show a little respect."

"No, mother. I can see your hand in this whole thing and your plan isn't going to work. You may think that a cop isn't good enough for me, but you're wrong. I love Eric, and I don't plan on going anywhere." Putting my arm around Eric and Abby, I told Brody that he should just leave before things got worse.

"I think I'll stay," he smirked. "After all, I did pay for a ticket to get in to this…thing."

"This thing?" Eric growled. "This 'thing' is something Karen has poured her entire heart into for the past month. Have a little respect."

"How about this," Brody asked, handing me an envelope.

Opening it up, I pulled out a check for one million dollars. "Are you trying to bribe me?" I spat, shoving the check back into the envelope, hoping Eric hadn't seen it. The look on his face told me otherwise. "I don't want your money."

"Move back to Cali with me, and I'll open you ten of your little shelters," he persisted.

"I'll manage just fine without you." Turning to walk away, I felt a hand grab ahold of my arm. Before I could spin around and tell him to let me go, I felt Eric grab him and put his hands behind his back.

"Time for you to leave," he said, leading him toward the door. "Don't make me radio in harassment and ruin Karen's party."

"She wouldn't have to throw these pointless parties if she would get her head on straight and be with someone of her status," he yelled over his shoulder as Eric continued to lead him toward the doors.

"Stop this right now!" I heard my mom shriek, drawing attention from nearby guests. "Karen!"

"No mom, he isn't welcome here. I don't know why you brought him in the first place."

After Eric had escorted my ex to the front doors and instructed the doorman not to let him back in, he returned and lead me out onto the dance floor away from my steaming mother, who was still going off on me.

"Okay, so I think you need to explain a few things for me," he began, once we were away from everyone. "First of all, your ex has a million dollars to just throw around? And what did he mean about being with someone of your status?"

"Um, well." I honestly didn't know what to say. My head was spinning in a million directions and I felt like I was going to be sick. "Can we talk about this another time?"

"I would really like to get everything out in the open now, but if you think it would be better to wait, you can explain everything after the party."

"Thank you," I whispered, leaning my head onto his shoulder as we swayed around the dance floor. "And I'm really sorry."

After the song finished, we cut across the room to find Trish and Abby. It was almost time for the dinner to be served, so I motioned for Trish to announce for everyone to find their seats.

Trish, clueless as to what had just gone on, made her way up to the stage and tapped on the microphone.

"Excuse me everyone? If you could all find your seats we are about to serve dinner. Thank you."

Returning to the table and sitting next to Abby, she leaned toward me and asked what was going on.

"Nothing," I mouthed. "I'll tell you later."

So far, my night was going nowhere near as planned. Glancing around I was relieved to see everyone else having a good time. Obviously the spectacle hadn't drawn too much attention or ruined anyone else's night.

My mother must have been too upset to stay, as right before our table was served, my dad was the only one who joined us. Acting like nothing had happened, he joined in our conversation and shot me a smile. He had always been good at letting things roll off his back.

As soon as dinner was over, I gathered everyone up and told them to go and start getting dogs ready. Before heading into the kennel myself, I announced into the microphone that we would now begin the debut of the dogs.

Looking to the left of the stage, I saw everyone lined up with their dogs and motioned them to begin. Trish was first in line with one of the new dogs, Tiny. Returning the microphone to its stand, I walked off the stage and watched as she lead the dog to the middle and began reading his bio.

Hurrying to get my own dog, I stood at the back of the line behind Abby, excited to get to see her work her magic with Rose on stage. Holding my breath and hoping the dog would cooperate, I watched in awe as she got the dog to immediately sit and then lay down while she read her short description to the crowd.

After all the dogs had made their way through the show, I slowly led Jaxx up onto the stage.

"Jaxx," I began, "has a special story. He was rescued from a dog fighting operation a few months ago along with several other dogs here. Having spent his life on the end of a 25lb chain, and trained to fight other dogs, he is currently not up for adoption due to behavioral issues. While Jaxx is not good around other dogs, he loves to get attention from people, and is a complete sweetheart once you get to know him. Recently we found out that he has heartworm, however, we caught it early enough to where treatment should have him back to his normal crazy self soon. If anyone would like to sponsor Jaxx or any of our other dogs that are not available for adoption yet, please fill out one of the sponsorship envelopes in the center of the tables. Thank you."

Jaxx, clearly feeling better and enjoying all the attention, decided to end the ceremony in his own special way. Just as the crowd began to clap, he threw his head back and let out an awkward howl, bringing everyone to their feet.

I handed the happy pit bull off to Trish and returned to the center of the stage. "Dessert will be served shortly, until then you are all welcome to close out your bids before we announce the winners.

I hadn't been around to look at what people were willing to pay for items in my collection, so when Trish began collecting the papers and handed them to me in a neat stack, I was shocked to see some of the things go for double what I expected. Once all the items up for auction were collected and brought up to the stage, I returned to the middle to begin announcing the winners as Trish held up the piece to go along with the bid.

Looking out at the crowd as they anxiously waited to hear their names called off, I rattled my way through the list of items until I reached the last one. I didn't recall receiving a donation for an all inclusive Caribbean cruise for two, and looked at Trish to make sure there wasn't a mistake.

"The package is right here," she whispered, showing me the tickets.

Still confused, I looked down at the list to announce the winner. "Eric Carlisle." Shooting Eric a confused look, I saw him look around and then shrug his shoulders, indicating he was just as lost as I was.

Leaving the rest to the crew I had hired to handle the auction portion, I took the steps two at a time and rushed over to where Eric and my father were standing.

"What's going on?" I asked, seeing a smile creep across my dad's face.

"I was just telling Eric here that I was proud of him for standing his ground and fighting for my only daughter, and that you two better have fun on your trip to the Caribbean."

"You bid on this for us?" I asked, still confused. "I don't even know where the package came from, it just showed up."

Seeing my dad wink at me, I playfully punched him in the arm. "You bought the package, donated it and then paid for it again!"

"Like I said, I'm proud of you Honeybee."

"So proud that you let mom almost ruin the entire night?" I asked, still angry at what happened earlier.

"I had no idea she was going to show up with him. I waited for her at the airport and finally left so I wouldn't be late here. You can imagine my surprise when I pulled into the parking lot behind her and watched Brody get out of the driver side. I didn't have any time to stop her."

"So, when did you decide to get the cruise package?"

"Oh, I didn't buy that. I found it in your moms car, I'm guessing Brody bought it as another ploy to get you to leave with him. I simply asked one of the workers to find a sheet to start a bid on, and set it on the table."

"I guess I'm not the only thief in the family." Thanking him one last time before heading off to talk with the guests, I looked over my shoulder and gave him a wink.

The crowd began to thin out after the auction, so before the remainder of the guests left, I got up on stage to say a quick thank you.

"If I could get everyone's attention for a minute." I chirped into the microphone and then waited for the room to get quiet before continuing. I just wanted to take a minute and say thank you to everyone who showed up tonight, your support is greatly appreciated. I'm new to the rescue world, and seeing you all come together to support this cause has really given me hope for the future of Four Paws Dog Rescue. As one person, I can't do a whole lot, but as a community I think we can accomplish something amazing.

Thank you again for coming, and be sure to check us out if you're ever in the market for a new companion. Every dog adopted, means a new one can be saved!"

As the room cleared out, I joined Eric for one last dance before the band packed up to leave. "I think tonight turned out pretty well," I said as he wrapped an arm around my waist while we danced.

"Are you kidding me! This was a huge success. I hope you raised enough to do everything you talked about."

"My dreams are unlimited, but I think it will be a good start."

"Imagine what you could have done had you accepted your ex's proposal. A million dollars could have gotten you everything you wanted. Are you sure you made the right choice in choosing me?"

"Of course I'm sure. If you want to hear the whole story, join me for a walk tonight after all the guests are gone. I'll tell you everything."

A few classmates lingered after the party was over, and I made my way over to chat with them before kicking them out for the night. Trish was trying her best to keep up with them, and gave me a look of relief when I finally joined.

"Emma, it's nice to see you," I smiled genuinely at one of my old friends. She was never big into the party scene like I had been, so after high school we drifted apart. "I heard you just graduated from Yale?"

"Last summer," she smiled. "It was fun, but I'm glad to finally be done with school. I took the year off and start my new job in two weeks."

"I hope you enjoyed your break."

"I did. Thank you for sending me an invitation to your event, it was a lot of fun. Once I'm settled into my job, I will definitely be looking you up to adopt a dog. I really like those two, Rose and Lilly. If they're still around in a few months, I might just have to take the both of them."

"That would be perfect," I said, hoping she meant it. "They really need to find a home together."

"Give me time to get settled in, and I'll get ahold of you. Take care of yourself." Walking toward the doors, she turned around and nodded toward where Eric and Abby were standing talking to my dad. "Nice catch, by the way. Your taste in men has improved since I last saw you."

Looking over to where my perfect boyfriend and his daughter stood, I smiled when I realized how right she was. I had everything I wanted, and then some. Not even a million dollars could take them away from me.

CHAPTER 11

"So you told him everything?" Trish asked when she met up with me the next morning to begin the clean up.

"Everything," I smiled. "He was shocked, and then mad, but by the time our walk was over it was as if nothing had happened. He acted happy for me, and said he was sure I would do good things with my inheritance once I received it."

"I told you he wasn't the type to care if you had money or not," she replied. "I'm sure it gives you peace of mind knowing that he wasn't just with you to get rich though. I can see where you were coming from by not telling him right away."

"I do wish I had told him sooner, before the whole explosion with my mom and Brody. I still can't believe she had the nerve to bring him. I don't know if I'll ever speak to her again after that stunt."

"You know how she is. You'll forgive her and move on in time. I can't believe he offered you a million dollars to leave your boyfriend! Can you say jealous?"

"No kidding," I laughed, remembering his face when I turned him down. "I'm pretty sure he thought it was a done deal the minute he walked through those doors in his Loro Piana suit and blinged out Rolex watch."

"You should have asked him to donate the Rolex before turning him down," she laughed.

"I never even thought of that! Next time an ex tries to steal me away, I'll remember to strip him of all his jewelry first. Speaking of which, did you finish counting up how much we made?"

"Ticket sales came in at just over twenty thousand dollars, and between the auction and donations, were well over a hundred thousand as of right now. I still have a stack to add in however, plus the $10,000 Britany sent for the purse. I know your one set of Harry Winston earrings went for a lot, and I haven't added them into the total yet either."

"This place is going to be the nicest rescue anyone has ever seen when we're finished," I beamed. "Especially since I decided to take the Cadillac to a dealership to trade in for something that can fit dog crates and we can use to haul dogs around. Last time it was evaluated they offered fifty grand for it, I'm sure that I can find a used vehicle for a lot less than that so there's some more money to add to the total."

"Have you ever thought of buying some land outside the city and building a brand new facility? I mean, this place works, but it needs a lot to fix it up."

"I think I'm going to stay here for now, and as soon as I get my inheritance I'm going to turn the warehouse into a boarding facility and build the rescues new facility closer to Atlanta so I can pull more from the high kill shelters there."

"Did your dad mention anything about when you will finally get your inheritance? It's been what, almost three years now."

"I didn't ask him. He told me he was going to plan another trip down this summer to spend some time with me, so if nothing has happened by then I'll bring it up."

Most of the room had been cleared out by the vendors last night before they left, so all that was left to do was pick up the trash and sweep the floors. Soon it could return to its original purpose, as an indoor play room where the dogs could stretch their legs until the outdoor fencing was put up. Since most of the property the warehouse sat on was grown over with weeds, I would have to hire someone to come in and clear it out before the fencing company could do their job. That was at the top of my priority list now that the funds were available, along with putting doors leading to outside runs in all of the suites. There were still two other rooms to build in, and I planned on lining the exterior walls of the play room in suites as well. I wanted to utilize all the space I could to rescue more dogs.

Elaine and I were planning on making a trip to the shelter in Atlanta where the rest of the fighting dogs were being held. Now that the case was almost closed, I would be able to pull the dogs soon and I wanted her help in deciding which ones she thought could be rehabilitated. I wasn't set up to take all of them at the moment, so I would have to pick which ones to take and which to leave. It wasn't going to be an easy decision since those that were left behind would more than likely be euthanized, but I had to keep telling myself that I could only do so much.

It only took until early afternoon to clean the play room up, and as soon as we finished we began letting dogs out in pairs to play. It was nice to be able to relax and watch them run around and enjoy themselves. Since Rose and Lilly were the last pair to be let out, instead of sitting around supervising them we began knocking out the evening chores to free up our night so we could all go out and celebrate the events success once Eric arrived.

Just as we were getting ready to head out for the evening, Abby came running inside and informed us that a lady and her little boy was standing at the door and asked to talk to the owner.

"Can I help you?' I asked politely after opening the door to a distraught woman.

"My friend was at your event last night and told me I had to come right away and look at one of your dogs, I think she said his name was Jack," she said excitedly.

I couldn't tell if she was on the verge of tears or was just really excited, so having to tell her Jaxx wasn't available for adoption to a home with little kids wasn't easy for me to do. "I think your referring to Jaxx," I began hesitantly.

"Yes, that's what it was! Is he still here?"

"Yeah, but I'm afraid he isn't up for adoption at the moment. He was just diagnosed with heartworm and is currently going through treatment. He isn't really suitable for a home with kids either I'm afraid."

"I don't think you understand. I'm pretty sure you have my dog!" Digging through her purse she snatched out a picture and handed it to me.

It certainly did look like Jaxx, but there was no way this could be the same dog. A lot of pit bulls had similar markings, and it was probably just a case of mistaken identity, but to ease her mind I lead the way through the kennel to where the sleepy pit was curled up on his blanket at the back of his room.

"Brutus!" she choked, holding back tears.

As soon as the dog heard the womans voice he jumped up and came running to the gate. Immediately upon seeing her, he began jumping up and down whining, doing everything in his power to get out of the room.

"That's my Brutus!" she said, grabbing ahold of my arm excitedly.

"How is this possible," I said, more to myself than the ecstatic woman. "How long have you been missing him?"

"He was stolen out of my yard when he was less than a year old," she replied. "Next month will be 2 years that he's been missing.

"I can't believe this."

"He has a scar on his back leg from cutting it on the fence trying to get out to chase a cat," she told me. "If you don't believe me than look."

"I don't have to look, his reaction is telling me everything I need to know. I just…"

"What?" the woman persisted. "Please let me see my dog."

Opening the door to the suite, I let the woman and her son in and watched as Jaxx jumped up and began licking their faces. The entire time his tail never stopped wagging. He didn't even greet me like that, and up until today I was his favorite person.

"Can we take him home? I'll pay whatever you want." Trying to get to her feet, the overjoyed pit knocked her back down and began showering her in kisses again.

"It isn't about the money," I began. "There's a lot you need to know about him. He isn't the same dog that you once knew."

"What do you mean he isn't the same dog. Isn't it clear that he remembers us and wants to come home!" she demanded.

I could see frustration building in her eyes as I tried to explain how he came to end up here.

"A fighting dog? There's no way. He used to go to the dog park and play with tons of other dogs there. He would never hurt a fly," she argued in disbelief. "Maybe someone got their stories mixed up."

"I'm the one who rescued him from the fighting operation. He was chained up in the woods with a dozen other fighting dogs," I explained calmly, trying to reason with the woman. "He can't even be walked near another dog without losing his mind."

"What do I have to do to get him back?"

"Do you have any other animals in the house now?" I asked, fearing she would say yes.

"We adopted another dog a year after he went missing. He's older and really laid back so I'm sure there won't be a problem."

"He cannot go to a home with other dogs. He has the worst case of dog aggression I have ever seen."

"What if we got him training?" she asked, determined to take her dog home with her.

"I don't think even that will be enough. He has been trained to fight other dogs, it doesn't matter if they're young, old, black or white. If he so much as sees another dog he gets amped up. I can't let him go into a situation where he is going to fail. I'm truly sorry."

"So what? He has to live here the rest of his life? Stuck in a room where no one loves him?' She asked boldly, not taking his case serious.

"Trust me, if we could get him into a home we would. All I know is he can't go to one that already has existing animals in it. He is well cared for here, and gets lots of attention. Everyone here adores him. You and your family are more than welcome to come and visit any time. We have a huge indoor play room that you can hang out in, and soon there will be individual rooms with couches and televisions if you just want to come and relax with him. That's about the best I can offer at this time. We will continue to work with him and try to minimize his reaction towards other dogs, but he will never be placed into a home with other dogs."

"Well, I guess if we can come and visit that will have to do," she said sadly.

I could understand her frustration. When she had Jaxx, or Brutus, it sounded like he was an amazing dog, but circumstances change when a dog is forced to fight.

"Like I said, you're welcome any time. Our doors are always open when we're around. If you plan on coming in the evening, just give us a call to make sure were here," I said. Handing her a business card with my cell phone number on it, I lead and her son toward the door.

"What was that all about?" Trish asked once the lady had driven off. "Is Jaxx really her dog?"

"Yeah, I think so. He certainly recognized them." Climbing into the passenger seat of Eric's suburban I turned around to finish telling them what happen.

"Apparently he was stolen out of their back yard a few years ago. She really wanted to take him home, but they already have another dog and I told her there was no way he could go to a home with dogs."

"That's really sad," Abby muttered. "I can't imagine finding my dog all those years later, only to find out he couldn't come back home."

"I told them they could come and visit him any time they wanted, that about all I can do though."

Right in the middle of our dinner out, my phone rang and seeing my dad's number pop up, I excused myself from the table and took the call.

"Hey dad, what's up?" My dad never called just to chit chat, so I was curious as to his reason for calling.

"Betty is in the hospital again, her cancer came back. The doctors are saying it won't be long now, a week at most. I think you should come and say your good byes."

My heart ached for the little old woman. She had been in my life since I was just a little girl, and wherever my grandma was, Betty wasn't far behind. After my grandpa passed, my gram and Betty became inseparable, having both lost their husbands in the same year. I used to spend a lot of my summers at her house playing with her little Pomeranians. She treated those dogs like they were her actual children.

"I'll see what I can do, but it's going to be hard to get away with all the stuff I have going on here right now." I really did want to get out there and see her before she passed however.

"She specifically asked for you when I talked to her this morning," my dad continued. "I think you should make it a priority to come out."

"I'll see if Trish can cover for me at the rescue," I replied, knowing he was right. Betty had always been there for me when I needed someone to talk to, and if she needed me to be there for her in her dying days, I would do everything I could to make it happen.

"I knew you would do the right thing. I already bought your plane ticket, you fly out tomorrow evening. It's a round trip for one day, I knew you wouldn't be able to stay and visit for long."

"Thanks dad. I'll see you tomorrow night then."

Trish had known Betty and was devastated to hear that she wasn't doing well. "Of course I will take care of everything back here, you go and say your goodbyes."

"I owe you." I knew I could count on Trish, she seemed to have my back no matter what.

"Nonsense," she replied, "Betty was like a grandma to you, just be sure to tell her that I love and miss her."

"I will," I smiled at my best friend. "Now, who is ready for dessert?" I didn't want the unfortunate news I received to ruin the rest of the night for everyone else so I announced that I was treating them all to the best triple chocolate fudge cake around. I had stumbled across this little bakery a few months ago and it was only a block away from where we were having dinner. The dessert there was to die for, and every time I came to the area I made it a point to stop and try something new. So far, nothing topped their fudge cake.

Just as we were finishing up, the waitress came over and announced that the cake was on the house. "I was at your event last night, and I really appreciate everything you do. It was my first time attending something like that, and to be honest my husband and I have been shopping around for another dog. We had a breeder picked out and were supposed to go and look at puppies this weekend, but I think we want to adopt now instead."

185

"I'm glad you've changed your mind and are considering adopting, you won't regret it," I smiled.

"We actually really like one of the dogs you have, Star. Is there any way we can come by and see her this week sometime?"

"How does Wednesday or Thursday sound? I have to make a quick trip out of town but I'll be back middle of the week."

"That sounds great! I look forward to meeting her."

After the girl walked away, Abby gave me a high five. "I hope she takes her!"

"That reminds me, Rose and Lilly might have a home too. One of the girls I went to school with really likes them and is thinking about adopting them in a few weeks if they're still available." I really had my fingers crossed for them. Not every day did someone come looking for two dogs, let alone two adult pit bulls. This could be their once in a life time shot.

"That's great," Eric said as he took the last bite of his cake. "I hope it works out for them!"

While everyone else was finishing up their dessert, I sat back and looked around the table as everyone laughed and had a good time. I wouldn't trade simple nights like this for anything. I couldn't believe I had once thought that I had the best life ever when I was living it up out in California.

All at once it hit me. This is exactly what my grandma had wanted me to find, and even if I never saw a penny of my inheritance, I realized that I had gained something money couldn't buy. A family.

CHAPTER 12

I had always enjoyed flying in the past, demanding that I get a window seat so I could enjoy the view. This time, however, I was too tired to even bother with gazing at the clouds as we sliced our way through them. Leaning my chair back just far enough that it wouldn't bother the passenger in the seat behind me, I put on some headphones and dozed off. It seemed like the past week I had gotten no sleep, and even though the flight wasn't a long one, the much needed nap felt refreshing.

Scanning the lobby after the plane landed, I found my dad waiting for me among the crowd. The lobby was packed with anxious people scurrying about looking for their guests, making me relieved that I no longer lived this hustle and bustle city life I had grown accustomed to. Atlanta, even though it was still a major city, was nothing compared to L.A.

"How's she doing?" I asked as soon as I made my way through the crowd and reached my dad.

"I'm afraid not well. She is still coherent, but they're saying she could go at any time." Leading the way to where his car sat, still running, he opened the door for me and then hustled over to the driver side. "I have a feeling she has been holding on just to see you."

Not much was said between the airport and hospital. My mind was all over the place, barely able to focus on one thing at a time. While I worried about the dogs back home, I found myself thinking about all the memories I had shared with the little old lady that lay clinging to life in her hospital bed. Even though I was glad to be able to say my goodbyes, the thought of losing Betty was taking its toll on me.

"I'll let you go in alone," my dad told me once we had reached her room on the 8th floor. "Come find me in the lobby when you're done."

Slowly opening the door, I peeked in to see if Betty was awake and found her laying curled up on the bed. I wasn't sure if her eyes were open so I softly whispered her name, wondering if I should come back later.

"Come in honey," she said, voice so low I could hardly hear her. Trying to sit up, she extended a shaky hand towards me so I could help her. "I'm so glad you were able to come out."

I pulled the only chair in the room closer to her bed and sat down. "I wouldn't have missed it for anything. How are you feeling?"

"Tired," she breathed. "The medicine is keeping me comfortable though."

"I'm sorry I haven't come out and visited before now. I should have made time." Looking at the woman whom I had always considered my second grandma, I felt a pang of guilt at only visiting her now that she was dying. "Have the girls been up to see you a lot?"

"They came up the day after I was admitted and I haven't heard from them since. I think I may have made them mad." A smile crossed her face. "You know how they are, if it isn't benefiting them they want nothing to do with it. I guess visiting their dying mother wasn't important enough to drag them away from their busy lives."

I figured they wouldn't be up here much. Betty's two daughters, Kathleen and Cary, were exactly the same as my mother. Family didn't rank high on their priority list. "I'm sorry."

"I'm not," Betty coughed. "If anything it has made some of my decisions a lot easier. I knew when I came in here that I wasn't going home again, so my first night here I had my will revised. I want you to look it over for me." Pointing toward the table on the other side of the room, she motioned for me to go get it.

"I don't really know anything about this kind of stuff," I admitted as I scanned through the document. Turning to the second page I noticed my name was down as a sole beneficiary. "What is this?"

"Your father told me what you have been up to these past few years. He is extremely proud of you, and 1 so am I. I knew if I left my money to the girls, they would just blow it like they do their own and I worked too hard for it to go to waste like that."

It took a second before what she was saying sank in. "Wait, you're leaving me your money?"

"Not just my money darling. My entire estate. I have it all drawn up and it's in the paperwork. The only thing I ask is that you take Poppy and keep him the rest of his days. He is old and I don't want to see him go to people he doesn't know."

I couldn't believe what I was hearing. Betty wasn't nearly as wealthy as my grandparents had been, but she was by no means poor. Looking through the rest of the papers, I saw the estate appraisal and the rest of the assets. Before I could add it all up in my head, Betty must had noticed what I was doing and told me the amount and how she would like it spent. Half a million in total, fifty percent in which she wanted me to use to open a sanctuary for dogs where they could live out the rest of their lives like her Poppy. The other half could go toward whatever the rescue would need.

"I bet you didn't know this, but every single Pomeranian I have had over the past twenty years, have been rescues," she pointed out. "I never told anyone for fear they would ridicule me. I'm just glad that in my old age, I finally don't care what people think. I'm proud of you for standing up for something you believe in, don't ever let anyone tell you that you can't do something you put your mind to. I know your grandma would be so proud of you too. I wish she were here to see you."

"I don't know what to say," I choked, holding the tears that threatened to pour out at any second.

"Just promise me that you will never give up hope. This world can be a brutal place, but if you have something to hope for you will always find a way to make it through. Now that you have found what you we're meant to do with your life, don't ever let anyone stop you."

"I promise." Giving her a hug, I asked if there was anything I could do for her.

"Just take Poppy home with you and give him all the love he needs," she smiled. "And stay the course. Don't give up when things get rough, no one ever got to where they wanted by giving up."

I could tell she was getting tired so I helped her back into a comfortably position laying down. I wasn't sure if it was the medication or if she was finally giving up, but her breathing slowed right down as she relaxed into the bed. Saying goodbye, knowing it would be the last time, was harder than I could have ever imagined. I didn't want to stay and keep her awake, but at the same time I was struggling to walk out of that room.

Just as I was about to leave, a nurse came in to do her routine checks. Glancing back one last time, I saw my dear old friend close her eyes for what I imagined to be the last time.

Handing my dad the paperwork when I met him in the lobby, I told him that I thought she was gone. It wasn't until we reached the car that I finally let myself break down.

My flight didn't leave until the following morning, so I talked my dad into making a quick stop by one of the shelters before we headed back to the house. I had never been to the city shelter and wanted to see how big it was and talk to them about their statistics. Having been left Bettys estate, which sat on nearly twenty acres, I was throwing around the idea of selling the house on an acre and keeping the remaining to build a sanctuary on. Before any decisions were made, however, I would have to talk to Eric and see where he stood on the idea of ever leaving Atlanta. I already knew that Trish would be on board with moving back to California.

Pulling up next to the brick building, I saw signs indication that the dog intake and kennel area was in a separate building toward the back of the property. Walking around back, I could hear the dogs before I saw them, and it sounded like there were quite a few. Small outdoor runs surrounded the entire building, each holding two to three dogs. We tried our hardest at the shelter I worked at to avoid putting dogs together, so it struck me as odd that this shelter would do it so freely. Once in a while when we were past capacity, we would pair dogs up that we knew got along, but that was only a last resort.

After making it around the entire kennel, I finally found a worker and asked for some numbers only to be blown away with what she told me. The facility was set up to hold sixty dogs, but when doubled up they could hold over a hundred. Their average intake per week was upwards of two hundred dogs and with their adoptions being less than fifty a week their euthanasia rate was over fifty percent. I had never heard of a rate that high out of any of the shelters I was familiar with back in Georgia.

"Which breeds are you finding get euthanized the most here?" I asked, hoping it wasn't the same as back home.

"Pit bulls, followed by terrier and chihuahua mixes, and then probably lab or lab mixes," she replied grimly.

"Do you get a lot of bait dogs or fighting dogs show up here?"

"Not as many as the shelter half an hour north of us, but we get our fair share of them. Unfortunately, our behavioral evaluator has to fail seventy-five percent of them so they don't even make it to the adoption floor.

That was about all it took for me to decide that building a sanctuary out here in Betty's name was the way to go. We had a problem with fighting dogs in Atlanta, but nothing compared to what was going on out here from what I was being told. I would have to look into it more and make some additional calls to the other surrounding shelters, but if what this girl was telling me was true, they desperately needed help here.

"I think that's a great idea," my dad told me once I explained my new plans. "It would be nice to have you closer to home as well."

"I still have to run it by Trish and Eric, but I think they will jump right on board. Will that affect me getting my inheritance though? Since I was supposed to stay out of California in order to get it?"

"I think under the circumstances, it will be fine. I will talk to your mother about it tonight over dinner. Speaking of that, did you bring a change of clothes? Your mom reserved a table at LaRue, and you know you can't go there dressed like that."

"I only brought another set of shorts and tank top for the flight home. I didn't realize we would be going to a fancy restaurant."

Making a quick U-turn, my dad spun the car around and headed back in the direction we had just come from. He found a spot between two other cars and tactfully parallel parked in one quick motion. That was something I had never mastered and had to do a 5 point turn to get myself weaseled into places.

"Here," he smiled, handing me his credit card. "Don't take forever, were supposed to meet your mom in an hour."

It had been a long time since I'd been to any of my favorite designer stores, and to my surprise some of the staff at the one I walked into still remembered me. Rushing me some of the latest designs, they swarmed around me displaying a variety of dresses, shoes and hand bags.

It felt odd having people cater to me after being out of this lifestyle for so long, and to be honest I didn't think I liked it. Realizing how much time and money I must had spent in these places, I suddenly felt ashamed for even being there and quickly picked out a plain black dress and a pair of what I hoped would be the cheapest shoes. After paying for my new outfit, I found myself wishing my dad would have taken me to a cheap department store instead.

"That didn't take long," my dad chuckled as I climbed into the car. "Do you need to go anywhere else?"

"No, I got everything I need," I replied, still feeling ashamed at spending a couple hundred dollars on a dress that would probably only get worn once. "Let's just get this dinner over with."

I was in no way excited about being around my mother after the stunt she pulled the other night, and I hoped she didn't have any tricks up her sleeves tonight.

Relieved to find the house empty when we got there, I rushed up to my bedroom, which I hadn't been in since being exiled from the state, to get changed. To my surprise, everything I owned was packed up in boxed and stacked along the wall. I wished I had time to go through it to see what I had left that could be sold, but instead I threw the dress on and headed back out to the car.

"Why is all my stuff in boxes?"

"I haven't a clue." Putting the car in gear, my dad backed out of the drive way and we made our way up town to meet my mother. "I haven't been in your bedroom other than to pack up the clothes you wanted for the auction and it was the same as you'd left."

Figuring my mom must had packed it all up after her rant the other night, I wondered what she planned on doing with everything. Not that I wanted any of it, but I knew there were items of value in there and the rescue could always use more money.

"What is this dinner for anyway?" I asked suspiciously as we pulled up to the valet entrance.

"I'm just following orders," he replied as the valet opened our doors. "She said she wanted to have a family dinner out, so I didn't argue or ask questions."

Before I could ask any more questions, I spotted my mom standing at the front desk waiting impatiently for us to arrive. Glancing at my phone to see if we were late, I had to chuckle to myself when I found we were ten minutes early and she was still annoyed. There was simply no pleasing this woman.

I followed behind my parents as the hostess lead the way to our table and thanked her when my mother failed to say a word. It wasn't my first time at this restaurant, but after eating at fast food and cheap little diners for the past few years I had a new appreciation for the place. Chandeliers hung above every table, casting rays of light off the expensive crystal glasses filled with every kind of wine you could imagine. I knew this because I had tried them all in the past.

A woman dressed in an overly revealing gown sat at the table across from us, laughing obnoxiously at something her date had said. Watching her take a sip of her red wine, I thought of how I had looked and who had watched me as I had probably looked just as foolish as I found her to be now. I suddenly had the urge to spill her red wine down the front of her expensive white dress and watch her go into a hysteria over how much it had cost her. I found it ridiculous the way she carried herself, clearly thinking she was better than everyone else.

"Karen!" I heard my mom scold me. "Stop staring that's rude. Do you care to join us at this table?"

Not really. I didn't care to be anywhere near this place to be honest. "I was distracted," I replied flatly.

"Obviously." Taking a sip of her wine, she looked at me over the rim of the glass. "Were you planning on attending a funeral in that dress? You could have at least attempted to look like you still have some class."

Annoyed that she had already found something to pick at, I asked what the dinner was for so we could get on with it. I figured it had something to do with the other nights events so I just wanted to get it over with, let my mom say what she needed to say, and go home.

"We just want to make sure you realize the decisions you are making before it's too late," my mom said, speaking for both her and my father.

I knew that wasn't how my dad felt, but decided not to call her out on it since that would only cause trouble for him. Instead, I calmly explained that I was happy with my decisions and that getting back with Brody was out of the question. This only added to my mom's frustration.

"Why aren't you using your head?" she scowled, looking at my dad for help. "That cop can't provide you with a life like Brody could, they don't make hardly enough money to support themselves. Plus, he already has a kid, do you really want to be raising someone else's child? You're not even mature enough for something like that."

"How would you know what I can or cannot handle?" I demanded, causing several people to look at us. Lowering my voice back down I told her to mind her own business and that I was happy with my life and didn't need her interfering.

Just as she was about to start in on another rant, the waitress came around with our food and began passing out the plates. I was relieved that my mom had enough class to keep her mouth shut until the woman walked away.

"Well it sounds to me like you have everything figured out and don't need any help, including your inheritance."

"Julia," my dad finally stepped it, "don't be ridiculous. Just because she isn't doing exactly what you want does not give you the power to decide something like that."

"The whole reason you're mom put us both in charge of deciding when she gets the money is because she knew how much of a push over you were. She won't get the money until she has her head on straight."

"We will talk about this later," my dad growled. Clearly unhappy with the way his wife was acting, he shoveled food into his mouth until his plate was empty. "Karen, whenever you're done we can head out."

Even though I had barely touched my food, I stood up and lead the way to the door. Glancing behind us, I saw my mom still sitting at the table sipping her wine with a smug look on her face.

"I'm sorry you got dragged into the middle of all this." I told my dad once we pulled up to the house. "I don't mean to cause all this trouble and then leave you here to deal with it alone."

"She is being unreasonable. I've tried to talk to her about this very matter several times and she just blows it off and says you're not ready for that kind of money yet. I disagree, I think you're more than ready and if it were up to me I would cut you the check right now. Unfortunately, she has just as much control over the account as I do, but I'll figure something out. Your grandmother would be proud of you."

I left my parents to talk once my mother stormed into the house an hour later, and headed up to my bedroom for some peace and quiet. My flight was scheduled to depart at six in the morning, and I still had to pick up Bettys Pomeranian from the boarding facility. Waiting for them to quit arguing, I began digging through the boxes that my mom had decided to pack my belongings into.

I was just putting everything back into one of the boxes when my dad peeked into my room and told me to go wait in the car and that he would be out in a minute so we could head over and pick up Poppy. Based on the shade of red his face was, I gathered their talk had not ended well so I avoided running into my mom by taking the east side stair case that lead down to the pool room instead of the main stair well.

"I don't know what that woman's problem is lately, but it's getting old." My dad mumbled as he slammed the car door shut. "Don't worry though, you're going to get your money."

"Did she agree to it?" I asked doubtfully.

"No, but I have another plan."

CHAPTER 13

After explaining my plan over dinner, as I suspected everyone was onboard with transitioning the rescue to California. Eric said he could transfer to a police department out there and since he had full custody of Abby there would be no issues with her moving out of state either. Trish was also more than willing to transfer to a different veterinary school to finish out her last few years.

On the plane ride back, I had tossed around a few ideas and jotted them down on a notebook I had picked up at one of the airport stores. The house could be sold for enough money to cover the costs to build a decent size facility, along with another building that would serve as apartment housing for us all to live at. There would be plenty of property left over for future development as well, which I planned to use a portion of to open Trish her own practice once she was out of school. Pulling the notebook out of my carry-on bag, I handed it to Trish to take a look at the drawings I had thrown together of what the facility could look like.

"I also have some other good news," I announced excitedly.

Trish's face lit up. "You got your inheritance didn't you?"

"My mom still won't sign off on it. However, my dad has found a way to work around it. He is going to send me a set amount each month out of his own paycheck, and when I finally get the inheritance I can pay him back."

"That's better than nothing," Trish replied. "What was your moms excuse for still not signing off?"

"She said I'm not thinking straight and am not mature enough to handle that amount of money."

"That's a joke," Trish muttered. "She just wants to dictate your life and is mad that using the money as a bribe isn't working."

"Dad's on board, so that's all that matters."

"When are you planning on doing this transition?" Eric asked.

"As soon as everyone is ready. How long do you think it would take to transfer to a police department out there?" I started picking up the table so we could go spend some time with the dogs before everyone had to go home for the night.

"It shouldn't take long, plus I have a lot of vacation time saved up so if I have to I can use some of that while waiting for the transfer."

"I have the summer off," Abby piped in excitedly as she jumped up to help me clean.

"I know you do!" I laughed, glad to see she was excited. I was afraid she would be hesitant to leave her school and all her friends, but that wasn't the case at all. "You will get to help us a lot this summer."

I planned on making some phone calls tomorrow afternoon to get the ball rolling, and since my dad was friends with a lot of realtors, there would be no problem getting the house sold. As soon as that happened the facility and apartments could start being built and we could move out there. Housing in that area of California sold extremely fast since it was outside of the city, so I wanted to have everything in order to move quickly. The biggest challenge I was faced with at this point was transporting all the dogs, especially since I had every intention of taking all the dogs from the fighting case in now that I had the funds. Elaine had called just as my flight landed and informed me that the case was closed and the dogs were now the property of the shelter and could be picked up at any time.

Even though we weren't set up to take in a dozen dog aggressive dogs, I was determined to make a way. So, tomorrow morning while Eric was at work, Trish and I were planning on moving kennels around and picking up a few more to put in separate rooms for when we went to pick the dogs up the following evening. It wouldn't be ideal, and they wouldn't get a whole lot of interaction, but it would have to suffice until we made the transition to California. Once we were out there, I planned on developing a program for volunteers to work with building the dogs trust back up. I didn't know if they would ever be able to get adopted, but they would always have a home with us. I also had every intention on hiring several people to help out at the kennel so all dogs would get the attention they needed.

Since it was a work night for Eric, he headed home right after we finished getting the dogs out for exercise. Trish made herself a bed on the couch, which Annie took over, and Abby climbed in my bed next to Posh and Ace. It wasn't a rare occurrence for everyone to spend the night at the facility with me anymore, and I had thought about making one of the other rooms into a separate bedroom so we weren't all cramped up in my little apartment, but with the new plans to move it was pointless to put all that work into it just to leave in a month or so.

I heard my alarm clock go off and bolted out of bed before it woke everyone else up. I had set it a little early so I would have a chance to spend some time with the dogs before the crazy day ahead of us consumed all my attention. After throwing some old work clothes on, I headed out to the kennel and made my way through all the rooms. I was only able to sit with each dog for a few minutes, but it was nice to spend one on one time with them since I hadn't had been able to in a while.

Curling up next to Jaxx, I wondered if his newly found family would come by and see him now that they knew where he was. It made me sad to think that just after their reunion, I would have to take him away when we made our move. As if he could read my mind, the big teddy bear of a pit bull laid his head in my lap and let out a sigh. He always did this when something was bothering me, like he was saying everything was going to be alright.

"You always know how to make me feel better," I murmured to the sweet dog as I gently ran my had across his neck. Hearing me talk he lifted his head up and looked at me with those piercing gold eyes, like he understood everything I was saying. "You will love it out there in Cali, I promise."

I was letting myself out of the last kennel when I heard a muffled voice coming from one of the rooms. Peeking into each one as I passed by, I stopped outside of Shadows room and listened to the little voice quietly talk to him. Not wanting to interrupt, I silently stood there until I heard Abby stand up and begin walking towards the door. Quickly letting myself into Roxy's suite, I watched as Abby made her way over to visit with another one of her favorite dogs. Leaving her to do her thing, I smiled as I walked past the room where she sat talking gently to Bear.

Drawing my phone out of my pocket, I dialed Elaine's number to set up a time to meet with her.

"Hey Elaine, what time do you want to head over to Atlanta tomorrow?"

Bursting through the door, Trish apologized when she saw I was on the phone and waited for me to hang up before telling me that the lady from the bakery was here to look at dogs.

"Have her come in. I'll be out in just a minute if you want to start the tour without me." Quickly measuring out kibble, I finished the last few bowls of food and then met up with Trish and the woman.

Surprised to find Abby leading the tour, I followed quietly behind the group and let her continue as she made her way through the row of dogs.

"Did you see any you liked?" she asked once the tour was over and they were back to the first room. "You can take them into the play room if you want to get to spend some time with any in particular."

She was like a little professional at doing tours, and you couldn't help but feel excited watching her face light up when she talked about each and every dog they passed.

"I liked a few of them," the woman smiled. "I don't remember all their names though."

"That's okay," Abby chirped, "We can walk back though and you can show me which ones."

Halfway down the row, the woman stopped in front of Stars room and said she would like to see her, so I grabbed a leash and told Abby to go ahead and take her to the play room.

"She's a natural," Trish said, as we watched the eleven year old lead the woman and the dog into the room as if she had been doing this her entire life. "She knew everything about every dog, and took over before I could get a word in."

Standing outside the room, we watched through the window as the woman threw a ball for Star to chase. They seemed to click immediately, even with Abby in the room. Since she was the main person that worked with Star, I figured the dog would completely ignore her potential adopter and was relieved to find I was wrong.

After a few minutes, Abby joined us outside and informed me that she thought they would make a great family.

"Did she say if she wanted to see any of the other dogs?" I asked.

"I don't think she does, she said she really likes Star."

Leaving them to bond, we began passing out the morning feed that I had ready and waiting. After all the dogs had their bowls slid into their rooms, I sent Abby to go check on the woman. Returning a few minutes later, she said they were laying together on one of the couches and that she was sure Star had found her new home.

Having seen people click with dogs at the shelter, and then leave without them, I knew better than to get my hopes up. Hoping to avoid her heart getting broken if Star didn't get adopted, I told her that sometimes what we feel isn't the same as what the other person feels and that an adoption is never for sure until the papers are signed, and even then dogs can get brought back. I found out rather quickly that you had to have some thick skin to work in animal rescue. Sometimes an adoption goes perfectly, and then other times it doesn't and the dogs are returned. All you could do is hope for the best.

As we were returning Star to her kennel, I heard a faint knock come from the front door and excused myself to go see who it was. Leaving the woman to talk with Trish and Abby, I stepped outside and was shocked to see a family standing there.

"Are you here to look at the dogs?" I asked, surprised at how fast the word had gotten out after the event. Over the past few days I had already received several phone calls from potential adopters wanting to stop by and look at our dogs.

The older woman took a step toward me and extended a hand for me to shake. "Our dog just passed away last month, and we've been looking around for another. A friend of ours told us about you guys so we figured we would stop by and see what you have. We're not really looking for anything in specific, our last dog was a mix, not really sure of what though. We would like a younger dog however, but not a puppy."

"Well, most of the dogs we have here are young to middle aged so you have a lot to choose from. I have some things that need my attention, so I'm going to have Abby give you a tour and I'll catch up with you shortly." Calling Abby over, I asked if she would mind doing another tour so I could finish up Stars adoption.

"Right this way." Rounding the family up, Abby lead them into the kennel to begin showing them the dogs.

With Star gone, and another dog possibly on its way to a new home, we would only have to pick up another three kennels to fit all the new dogs that would be arriving tomorrow. The family was interested in one of the smaller pit mixes I had rescued off the euthanasia list a few weeks ago, but wanted to think about it for the night and get back with me in the morning.

Once all the kennels were put up throughout several different rooms, we called it a night and Trish headed home leaving Abby and I to spend the evening together. I couldn't remember the last time I stayed alone at my house, and was thankful for the little girls company. It made living in a run down old warehouse not seem quite as bad.

"Why don't you pick out a movie, and I'll grab some dogs." I told her as I made my way towards the door. "I'll be right back."

There were a few dogs that I wanted to introduce to my growing pack that stayed with me in the apartment at night, but seeing how it was only the two of us there I decided to only introduce one of them tonight. Grabbing a leash on my way through the kennel, I let myself into Midgets room and slipped the rope over his head. Since bringing Betty's little Pomeranian, Poppy, home with me, I felt like they would get along great since they were close to the same size. Posh wasn't that much bigger, but still a little too rough for Poppy's taste so I hoped Midgets calm demeanor would help the Pomeranian adjust to his new life with us.

Midget looked up at me confused, as I led him through the room and towards my apartment. His calm and submissive personality had lead me to believe that he wouldn't be here very long, but so far he had no interest from any of the potential adopters. Gently picking him up, I carried him into the apartment so he wouldn't get overwhelmed when the six other dogs excitedly met us at the door. Poppy tended to stay away from the pack when they got excited after already being stepped on by dancing feet, so I waited for everyone to calm down before setting Midget down next to him.

Completely ignoring the new dog, Poppy wandered off to his corner and curled up into a ball in his bed, leaving Midget standing there alone. Looking around at all the other much bigger dogs, it didn't take but a few seconds for him to wander over to the quiet corner with the grumpy old Pomeranian and hesitantly lay down next to the bed.

"Do you think they will eventually be friends?" Abby asked, watching the two little dogs completely ignore each other.

"Poppy is still adjusting, he should be fine in a few days and ready to socialize. I think the two of them will do great together once he comes out of his shell."

Curling up on the couch among Abby and the rest of the dogs, we began our movie and settled in for the night. Mid way through, after dozing off several times, I faintly heard my phone ring from across the room. Wondering who would be calling this late at night, I scurried from beneath the pile of dogs and peacefully sleeping child and got to my phone just in time to answer the call.

"Hello?" The number was one I hadn't seen before, which only added to my curiosity.

"Is this Karen?" The unfamiliar voice asked.

"Yes. Who is this?" Stepping out of the room so I wouldn't wake Abby up, I waited for a response.

"I got your number off the rescues website and I was hoping you could help with something. There's a dog wandering around the neighborhood and it looks sick, but no one has been able to catch it."

I had never really done any hands on rescue work, that was always animal controls job. "Have you contacted the local shelter? They will send someone to catch the dog."

"Ma'am, the dog is a pit bull. I don't want animal control getting their hands on him."

I could understand that, since the breed rarely made it out of the shelter. "Where are you located and when was the last time you seen the dog?"

He gave me an address, which was only about half an hour away, and told me that it was in his yard now. I couldn't help but feel like I had to do something. He continued to tell me that the dog was way underweight and seemed to be limping on one of his back legs, and if someone didn't catch it soon it would probably end up dying.

After hanging up, I quickly woke Abby up and told her to get dressed and help me put the dogs away. Scooping Midget up from where he lay sleeping, I noticed that Poppy had made room in his bed and the two were actually laying in it together.

"What's going on?" Abby asked once she had changed out of her pajamas and began helping me get the dogs returned to their rooms. "Is everything okay?"

"Were going to go for a little drive," I explained, hoping Eric wouldn't mind. "There's a dog that needs our help."

"Were actually going to go out and save a dog!" She replied, instantly going from half asleep to fully awake. "Where is it? What's wrong with it?"

I relayed what the man had told me and watched as her face grew more and more excited. "I can't believe we are actually going to save its life! This is awesome! Well, I mean not that the dog is suffering, but just getting to be the ones to save it is pretty cool."

I felt my adrenaline begin pumping as we got closer to the address I had punched into GPS. Realizing I hadn't felt this way since the nights I stole the dogs off the neighbor's property, I began to wonder if brining Abby along was the right thing to do. It was different this time though, I wasn't doing anything wrong and it would be good for her to watch from a distance so that one day she could help.

Pulling into the drive way, I saw the man standing on the porch with his back to me. Scanning the yard for the dog, I told Abby to come with me to look since we were in an unfamiliar neighborhood and I didn't want her staying in the vehicle alone.

"Is the dog still around here?" Standing on the porch steps, I waited for the man to turn around.

Motioning for us to join him, he pointed to what I figured was the dog so we slowly walked across the porch to get a better look. Only, it wasn't the dog I noticed, but an open screen door that led into a very unkempt house where a girl sat smoking a cigarette at the table. Suddenly feeling uncomfortable, I was just about to turn around when someone stepped out behind us.

"Abby run!" I yelled, as soon as the strangers face came into view and I recognized him. Hovering above us stood the man who had shot me the night I attempted to rescue Annie.

Before Abby could move, the man pushed the two of us through the screen door then grabbed me by the arm and began dragging me down a hallway.

"I knew you wouldn't be able to resist coming out here if I said there was a dog needing your help," he smirked. "You made it way too easy. Having a little kid with you, that wasn't in the plan however."

"What do you want!" I screamed, struggling to free my arm from his grasp. Using every ounce of strength I had, I slammed my body into his hoping he would stumble and let go.

"I told you, I want our dogs back." Opening a door to what looked like a basement, he shoved me into the dark, cold room and then slammed it shut. A few moments later I heard the door knob unlock and the door open as the man pushed Abby in and told her to be quiet.

Seeing her tear soaked face, I wrapped my arms around the frightened girl and told her that everything would be okay, even though I didn't know how. Instead of standing on the steps helplessly, I lead the way down to the basement to look for a way out, or a weapon of some sort to use next time the door was opened.

Flipping the light at the bottom of the stair case, it took a moment for our eyes to adjust to the brightness. The room illuminated instantly with rows of lights for as far as I could see, and what lay hidden in this secret chamber made me instantly sick to my stomach.

I recognized the fighting ring right away. The floor was stained red from the blood where countless fights had taken place only feet from where we were standing. The sight made me throw my hand over my mouth to keep the vomit down as I turned Abby away from the revolting scene.

"This is where they fight them isn't it?" she sobbed, burring her face into my chest. "What is going to happen to us!"

"We're going to get out of here." Determined to stay true to my word, I began searching for a door that lead out. If this was where they held the fights than there had to be another exit other than through the house. Tiny windows lined the top of the walls, with black tarp taped over them so no one could see in. Ripping the tarp off of one of them, I sighed when I saw how small it actually was. There was no way either of us were fitting through them, especially since they were 5 feet off the ground and I couldn't even see out let alone lift Abby up that high.

Looking around for another way out, we eventually found a door that I hoped would be an exit. Knowing it would be locked, I tried the handle anyway and was shocked when it turned. Quietly as I could, I opened the door just enough to peek though in case someone was out there waiting.

It was another room, not an escape.

Opening the door all the way, I jumped back when I heard an eruption of barking come from within the dark. Slamming the door shut, I leaned my back against it and caught my breath.

"There are dogs in there!" Abby exclaimed.

"By the sounds of it, there are a lot. It's more than likely where they're keeping their fighting dogs since they just got busted not too long ago. Smart."

The barking stayed the same, not getting louder like it would if the dogs were able to get close to the door. Quietly opening it again, I peeked my head through and made out a row of cages lining both sides of the walls. It was too dark to see how many dogs were in there or if they were all in cages.

"Stay here," I demanded as I slowly walked into the room and looked for a light switch. Hoping all the dogs were contained, I softly spoke to them trying to quiet their barking so no one would come looking for us.

Finally, after what felt like an eternity of searching for the lights, I found a string hanging from the ceiling just to the left of where I had walked in. Pulling it, I felt the switch catch as one single bulb turned the room into a soft glow of yellow light. Lighting the room up just enough to see, I looked around to get a better feel for my surroundings.

Four sets of eyes peered at me from behind their rusted metal jail cells as they continued to bark at the intruder. Motioning Abby in, they erupted into another frenzy of barking when she walked over next to me.

"Shhh," Abby said quietly as she bent down in front of one of the dogs cages. "We're all getting out of here."

The girls voice slowly began calming the dog as she kneeled next to the cage and softly spoke to him, promising him that it would be okay.

Leaving her there to calm the rest of the dogs down, I began searching for another way out. Chains and leather contraptions lined the cobb web filled walls as I searched deeper into the room looking for another door. When I finally found what I was looking for, my heart sank as I tried turning the door handle. I should have figured it would be locked. The only thing between us and freedom, was this deadbolted door.

CHAPTER 14

I wasn't sure what our kidnapers tactic was, but keeping us locked in a basement wasn't bringing them any closer to getting their prize winning dog back. One, that I might add, they had stolen from a loving family as a puppy. I had locked the warehouse up before we left, and short of using a bulldozer to get in, there was no other way. Every entrance door had double heavy duty locks, and I always made sure they were fastened before I left. Not only that, but the entire lot was also surrounded by a six foot tall chain link fence, with a locked gate that secured the drive way. The only time that was locked was at night, but in our rush to get to the stray dog I couldn't remember if I had shut it or not. My concern wasn't in them breaking into the facility, but rather how anyone would find us here locked in a basement half an hour away. Even with Eric's police skills, it would be a shot in the dark.

The morning sun poured in through rips in the canvas that covered the windows as I searched the room for something to stand on to see out. Even if I could get up that high, there was no way I could fit through one. Abby was just a little smaller than me, however, and might be able too if I could hoist her up that far. Uneasy about sending her off alone, I couldn't think of any other way to get help.

"Help me drag this empty crate over here." Waiting for her to pick up the other end, I glanced back at the door to make sure we were still alone. I was sure the dogs would alert us to when someone was coming, but that didn't stop me from constantly looking over my shoulders.

Once the crate was under the window, I gently crawled on top of the wobbly wire contraption and wondered if it would hold me if I stood up. While on my hands and knees, my weight was more evenly dispersed, but the moment I tried standing the crate began to cave in. Grabbing for the window ledge, I took some of the weight off just before it gave out entirely and sent me crashing to the floor. Beads of sweat began forming on my face as I realized that any form of commotion would send the dogs barking and possibly alert our kidnappers that we were up to something.

Gaining my balance back, I leaned forward and wiped the cobwebs away from the window so I could see out. The sunlight was blinding and it took a while before my eyes adjusted well enough to make out the lay of the yard. It was hard to see much with how over grown the grass was, but I could just barely make out a road not too far away.

The cover of the night would have been more ideal for sending her out in, but I didn't know how much time we had before they came back for us so I decided it was probably now or never. Hoping they had spent the night trying to get into the facility, I figured everyone would still be asleep and she could slip out unnoticed.

"All you have to do is make it to the road. Then run. Find a neighboring house and ask to use their phone. Call your dad and tell him this address." Making her repeat the address they had given me, I gave her a quick hug and reminded her to stay low to the ground and move quietly. "There is no one out there right now as far as I can see, but if that changes, the grass is tall enough, lay down and use it for cover. Remember, don't trust anyone and when you call your dad don't say anything other than the address. He will figure it out. After you talk to him, find a place to hide and watch for him to come. Don't try to get a ride with anyone. Do you understand everything I'm saying?"

Tears streamed down her dirty face as she nodded her head. "I understand."

Moving the crate out of the way, I hoisted her up so she could reach the window and climb out. As soon as she was out of the way I drug the crate back over and carefully balanced myself on top so I could watch as she followed my instructions and carefully made her way toward the road. Glancing around once she was out of sight, I took a much needed breath after seeing that she made it to the road without any sign of someone seeing her.

Now all I could do was wait. Wait and hope that she would be okay. After moving the crate back to where I had found it, I sat down with my back against one of the cages and let the pit bull trapped inside lick my hands. I knew eventually someone would come to take care of the dogs, and already had a story in place for when they did. Until they came, however, there was nothing I could do but sit there and wait.

As the time slowly passed by, I felt my eyes getting heavier and heavier until I finally couldn't keep them open any longer. Trying to keep myself from falling asleep, I wandered around the room pointlessly. I knew there was no other way out besides the door, and there was no point in wearing myself out trying to force it open. I would need what little strength I had left to fight off my kidnappers if that's what it came too.

What seemed like hours had already passed and I was growing more exhausted by the minute. Finally giving in, I slumped down against the wall on the other side of one of the kennels where I would be out of view and closed my eyes.

Hearing the dogs grow restless, I figured someone was nearby and found myself wishing that I had found a better place to hide. There was no time to go looking for a better hiding spot now, however, as the door leading to the kennel flew open just as I was about to stand up. Hoping who ever had come down here would just do a quick scan of the room and then leave, my heart began to race as I heard footsteps growing closer and closer with every beat of my heart. Suddenly they stopped. Slowly lifting my head up from between my knees, I looked my kidnapper dead in the eye.

"Where is she?" The man growled. Grabbing my arm, he whipped me up so fast I felt something pop in my shoulder. Where is the girl!"

Trying to ignore the pain that was coursing through my entire arm, I told him that we were playing hide and seek and she was hiding.

"Tell her the games over. We're moving to a different location in a few hours. Unless, you want to tell us how to get into the facility."

If they moved me to a different location, I would have no way of reaching Eric. He would show up here and I would be gone. They had more than likely already taken the keys out of my car and tried using them at the warehouse. The gate and facility key, however, were in my pocket so I knew the dogs would remain safe.

Without saying a word, I nodded towards the other room indicating that's where Abby was hiding. Following the man as he lead the way out of the kennel area, I quietly slid my hand into my pocket and drew out the nail I had found on the floor earlier. It wasn't much of a weapon, but it might buy me enough time to get out, granted the door at the top of the staircase wasn't locked.

Sliding the nail through the eye of my key, I placed it between two of my fingers, sharp edge sticking out, and made a fist. I waited for the man to turn around, and when he finally did I threw as hard a punch as I could and landed it right in his neck. Quickly pulling my hand back, I punched him again several times in the side and waited for him to fall to his knees. Gripping his neck with his hand to stop the blood, I saw my moment of escape and took it.

By the time I reached the steps, I could hear the man getting up and running after me. Halfway up the stairs, my foot missed a step causing me to fall face first, giving me kidnapper time to get closer. Quickly standing up, I reached the door and was relieved to find it wasn't locked. Bursting through it, I glanced around to see if anyone was there and then beelined it for the screen door at the end of the hallway. Just as I reached it, a girl grabbed me by the arm and impulsively I swung my hand toward her face. Even without the nail, I hit her hard enough to send her stumbling backwards into the table. If anyone else was in the house, I was sure to have their attention now.

Jumping off the side of the porch instead of taking the steps, I hit the ground hard and felt my knees give out beneath me. Hoping I hadn't broken anything, I got back to my feet and took off across the yard towards the road.

Between the lack of food and sleep as well as the heaviness from the humidity outside, I didn't make it far before having to stop and catch my breath. I could feel my lungs burning from beneath my chest as I gasped for air. I knew it wouldn't be long before someone caught up with me, so I began running again, this time at a considerably slower pace. Trying to push myself to move faster as I heard shouting come from behind me, I realized I had no more energy left and it wouldn't be long before I collapsed all together.

Glancing behind me to see if they were on the road yet, I darted off into a yard when I realized they were further back that I had though. I knew I wouldn't be able to out run them so I took the next best option and hid.

Several hundred feet off the road sat an old farm house surrounded by thick shrubs. Diving in between two of the bushes, I hid myself the best I could and watched for my kidnappers, hoping they hadn't seen me dart off the road. If I was lucky, they would run on by and I could see if anyone was home and use their phone.

It wasn't long before three men came into my view. None of them were running and I could just barely hear what they were saying to one another.

"If we don't find her soon than we have to get out of there. She's with a cop." I heard one of the men say.

"I'll go and start loading the dogs up. Where do you want me to take them? Back to Atlanta?"

I had to hurry and get ahold of Eric before they could move the dogs and make it impossible to find them again. I wouldn't live the rest of my life in fear of these men.

Patiently, I waited for them to get far enough out of view and then scurried up the porch and began frantically knocking on the door. When no one answered, I crawled back behind the bushes and waited, hoping someone would come home soon. I didn't want to leave my hiding spot to find another house, but somehow I had to get ahold of Eric. I knew they hadn't caught Abby or they wouldn't have asked where she was, but that didn't keep me from worrying.

Night was beginning to fall, and I couldn't bear the thought of leaving Abby all alone and afraid in the dark. Just as I was about to leave the comfort of my hiding place, I saw lights coming up the driveway. Waiting for the older couple to get out of their vehicle and disappear into the house, I quietly slithered from behind my cover and walked casually up to the porch.

"Can I help you?" The older man asked as he opened the front door.

"I just need to make a phone call. My car broke down up the road and I have to get ahold of my boyfriend."

My appearance must had given me away, as the man took one look at me asked how far up the road my car broke down. "You look like you've been walking for hours."

"Umm, well…" I began, trying to come up with an excuse for why I looked the way I did. Before I could come up with an answer, he handed me a cell phone and told me to come inside.

"It's ok," I replied, "it will only take a second."

Suddenly I froze as I came to the realization that I didn't even know Eric's phone number. The only persons number, besides my parents, that I had memorized was Trish and I knew she would panic if I called her. What choice did I have though.

"Trish," I said calmly, "You need to get ahold of Eric." Looking around to make sure no one could hear me, I gave her the address and told her that Abby and I had been kidnapped last night, but we were both safe for the time being.

"I don't have his number in my phone," she replied in a panic. "I stopped by the warehouse today and it was all locked up, I figured you guys had gone out for the night or something. I'm on my way though. I'll be there soon."

The last thing I wanted was for Trish to get involved and put herself in danger. I wished I knew where Abby was, I couldn't imagine the two of us out searching for her would end well with the kidnappers out on the hunt as well. It wasn't like we could walk up and down the road yelling her name.

"Thank you." I told the man as I handed the phone back to him.

"Would you like to come inside and wait?"

I wouldn't be entering any strangers home anytime soon, even if they were older. "No thanks, I'll just head back to my car and wait for him there."

Slowly walking down the steps, I waited for the door to close so I could dart back into my hiding place where I would wait for the next hour. Peeking out between the bushes thick branches, I watched as the night grew darker by the minute. Restlessness over took as I sat there and waited, feeling like my body would explode if I didn't get up and do something.

The road wasn't very heavily traveled, so every time I saw headlights I strained my eyes to see if it was Trish's car. Finally, after what I guessed to have been an hour, I crawled out from behind the cover of the bushes and made my way toward the road. Now that it was dark enough that I wouldn't be easily spotted, I sat down beside the mail box and waited for the next car to drive by.

Three more passed and not one of them slowed down. Finally, just as I was about to lose hope that she would ever find me, I spotted her car creeping up the road. Waiting for it to get closer, I stood up so she would see me once there were only a few feet in between us.

"I thought you were never going to find me," I said as I quietly closed the car door behind me to avoid drawing any attention.

Trish nodded toward the back seat, not saying a word. It was dark inside the car, so I really had to focus to see what she was directing my attention to back there. As soon as my eyes adjusted I could barely make out the shape of someone laying on the seat.

"I found her about two miles away." I didn't need to see Trish's face to tell that she was mad. Relieved, but mad none the less. "Karen, what were you thinking?"

"I don't know," I sighed. Looking back at the whole situation, I realized I should had done a lot of things differently.

"You can't just go on these crazy rescue missions in the middle of the night, with a child. Can you imagine what Eric is going through right now? He hasn't heard from you or Abby in over 24 hours. They probably have a search team out for you at this point."

The reality of what she was saying hit me hard as I blankly stared out the window. Even though my mind was going in a million directions, I knew the first thing I needed to do was call Eric. "Pull over once we get to town, I need to wake Abby up and get Eric's phone number."

Trying to think of what I was going to say once I finally had him on the line, my heart began racing at the thought of how he would react. I only hoped that he wouldn't be made enough to break up with me.

"Abby," I gently shook the little girls leg once we had pulled into a fast food parking lot. She stirred but didn't wake up, so I said her name again.

Slowly opening her eyes, she bolted straight up as soon as she recognized me. Climbing over the center counsel, she threw her arms around my neck and hugged me. I could feel tears dripping from her face onto my shoulder as she began to sob.

"Everything is okay now," I whispered, trying to comfort her as much as I could. "We're all safe."

"I couldn't call my dad. Every house I went to, no one came to the door so I just walked around in the woods until it got dark out."

"It's okay," I replied. "We can call him now."

Punching the numbers into Trish's phone as she gave them to me, I pushed the call button and took a deep breath.

The phone only rang once before a worried voice answered. "Hello?"

"Eric..." I began.

"Karen! Where are you? I have tried calling you all day!"

"I'm really sorry," I apologized, not knowing how to tell him everything that had happened. "I will explain everything. Can you meet us at the warehouse in an hour?"

"Yes, I'll be there. Is Abby alright?"

"Everyone is fine," I whispered. Feeling my eyes begin to well up with tears, I told him goodbye and slumped back into the seat exhausted.

It wasn't a few minutes after we got back on the road and I could feel my body begin to get weak. Glancing at Abby in the back seat, I relaxed once I seen her fast asleep, and closed my eyes giving in to the exhaustion.

Feeling my body being lifted from the seat, I jolted awake and looked around in a panic. My mind was still half asleep and began playing tricks on me as I whipped my head around to look in the back seat where Abby was no longer curled up in a ball. Yelling her name, I began fighting my way out of the grip of whoever had picked me up out of the car.

"You're fine. You're fine." I heard someone whisper. "Abby's inside sleeping."

It took a while for my mind to clear before I realized it was Eric who had lifted me out of my seat and was carrying me into the building. Gripping him tighter, I tried to hold back the tears as relief flooded through my body.

"Trish told me what had happened," he said as he put me down on the couch and then sat next to me.

"I'm so sorry. I know it was stupid what I did and I should have called someone before we left. I should have dropped Abby off at your house or Trish's house. I wasn't thinking straight. It will never happen again. I promise…" Cutting me off before I could babble any longer, Eric leaned my head onto his chest and silently held me.

After a while, he finally spoke. "I'm taking the day off tomorrow. We're going to sit down and figure out how to get out of here. Maybe your dad will give you enough money to get started on the facility until the house sells. Either way, you aren't staying here any longer. I don't think we're dealing with your average dog fighters, if they're willing to go the extent of kidnapping who knows what else they will do."

"I'll call him in the morning and see what he says. I'm sure he will help any way he can." I was too tired to think, let alone call my dad and explain everything. "Did Trish go home?"

"She is taking care of the dogs right now," he replied. "I think she is more shook up than any of us. I'm not making light of what happened, but it wasn't you're fault."

"She's mad at me," I whispered as guilt filled my mind once again.

"She will get over it. Like I said, it wasn't your fault. How could you have known any of this would happen."

I wanted to talk to Trish before she left for the night, but my body had other plans. As soon as I laid down and Eric began running his fingers through my hair, I passed right out.

CHAPTER 15

After talking to my dad and getting a plan in place, I made a few more phone calls then set to work packing everything I owned into boxes. The only thing left to take care of was transporting all the dogs, which I planned on finding a cheap bus for sale and fastening crates inside.

We would be moving into an unfinished facility, but my dad guaranteed me that the building would be constructed within a week and that was all I needed at this point. The rest would come with time. Having a place to house all the dogs was my only focus at the moment, and since I already lived in a warehouse moving to another wouldn't be that big of a deal.

Eric refused to leave the property without me, so when he went to put his notice in at the station we all tagged along and waited in the vehicle. There wasn't enough time for him to transfer departments, so the best he could do was offer a one week notice and then start over once we moved to California. I had mentioned working at the rescue full time, but his passion for police work was too strong to give it up.

"How did it go?" I asked once he returned to the car.

"They weren't happy to be losing me on such a short notice, but they understood and said I would receive a great recommendation once I found another station to work at."

Seeing the guilt on my face, he picked up my hand and flashed me a genuine smile. "I'm excited to start this new adventure with you."

"I'm excited too," I smiled, trying to push the remorse I felt for being the reason he had to move on a whim to the back of my mind.

"Not as excited as I am," Abby added from the backseat.

I had worried that after what happened, she wouldn't want anything to do with rescue anymore. That wasn't the case however. All she talked about now was getting those dogs out of the basement of the house.

Every part of me wanted to go back and rescue them, but I knew they wouldn't be there. Eric informed his higher in command what had happened, and they were going to reach out to that jurisdiction and send a team out to the house to check it out and recover my vehicle if it was still there.

"What are you excited for?" I asked her out of curiosity.

"A lot." She replied excitedly. "Getting to live at a rescue, and live with you."

Hearing her say that warmed my heart, and every doubt I had as to whether or not the past nights experience changed her mind about me or the rescue vanished.

"It's going to be a lot of fun," she added.

Stopping by the local store we used for most of the kennels supplies, we had the staff load the back of the suburban full of crates of various sizes. It was a shame we had to move after having just put all the time into remodeling the facility, but it was necessary.

"We gave you a discounted rate for buying so many," the woman told me at the checkout. "We're all really sad to see you leave."

I had never sat down and thought about how many relationships I had built within the community due to the rescue, and having to suddenly leave it all behind left an empty pit in my stomach. I only hoped that the new community we were moving to would be as welcoming as this one was.

"Did they have enough?" Eric asked once I returned from paying.

"I bought them out, so I hope so." Several of the dogs didn't need a crate as they would be riding in the suburban with me, and Trish had volunteered to take Posh and Poppy in her car. It was going to be a challenging trip with that many dogs and having to stop every few hours to let them out. Thankfully, we had a good size team between the four of us.

Later that evening, Trish met up with us at the warehouse and to my relief was in a much better mood. That was the best thing about our friendship, we never stayed mad at each other for long. Not once did she mention what had happened, other than to ask if the police had contacted us with any news.

Having a list of things we each had to accomplish, I set to work listing the facility for sale as a rescue or boarding facility. Wanting to get out from under it as soon as possible, I kept the price low in hopes that it would sell fast to help pay for our housing to be built.

I had been tossing a few ideas around inside my head all day, and waited until we were all settled in to mention them to the others.

"What do you think about setting up cabins?" I asked, as we all sat around the table. "They're already built and would only need the insides finished, and we would be able to put up several of them for the same amount it would cost to build the apartment complex we had planned on. The living spaces would be considerably smaller, however, that would leave us with a few extra cabins that could be used for some kind of volunteer program. Or we could use the extra ones to house some of the dogs that aren't adoptable, so they don't spend the rest of their lives in a kennel environment."

"It would definitely be more time efficient, which would help us a lot right now," Eric said after thinking it over.

"I'm used to living in a dorm room," Trish laughed. "It wouldn't be much of a change for me! I like the idea, and it's not like we spend much time sitting around at home anyway with how busy we are."

I could pay cash for three cabins to be put up right away with what was left over from the gala, which would keep us from having to live in the kennel facility when we made the move out there. I would have to contact the city and make sure it was legal before making any permanent decisions, but I didn't see why it wouldn't be.

We were all deep in conversation when Abby suddenly jumped up and ran to the door. I could hear her talking to someone once she stepped out, and my guard automatically went up sending me running over to join her.

My old boss, Elaine, stood talking to Abby in the door way and gave me a look of concern when I stepped out to join them.

"I have been trying to reach you for the past two days," she informed me.

With all the drama from the last few nights, I had totally forgotten that all the fighting dogs at the Atlanta shelter were supposed to be picked up the other day.

"They haven't been euthanized yet, have they?" I asked in a panic. How could I have forgotten about them!

"When I didn't hear from you the morning we were supposed to pick them up, I called the shelter and asked if we could have another day to get things set up. When I couldn't get ahold of you all day yesterday or today, I didn't know what to do. They're scheduled for euthanasia tomorrow morning, so if you still want them you better be there before they open at eight."

"I will be there," I replied. "Thank you for coming over, I lost my phone a few nights ago and a lot has been going on. I still can't believe I forgot about them though."

"You need to take a step back and catch your breath. You're pushing yourself into the rescue world to hard and too fast, it's only going to end with you getting burned out and not wanting to do it at all." Leaving me with this warning, Elaine told us goodbye and walked out the door.

Abby looked up at my confused. "What did she mean by that?"

"Nothing," I smiled, knowing exactly what my former boss had meant. "We just have to keep pushing forward and make sure we stay on track."

Lying in bed that night, Elaine's words swirled around in my head. Was I taking on too much? It sure felt like it at times, but it also felt like I had no other choice. My only option was to keep pushing forward.

Sleep didn't come easy, as I tossed and turned all night worrying about everything that was going on. With the new dogs we were taking on, that brought our number up to 35 plus mine and Eric's personal dogs, and Poppy. We would need more crates, which wasn't a big deal. My fear was space. The couple of bus's I had found for sale would only fit a certain amount of dogs, what if there wasn't enough room for all of them. Making a mental note to call all the potential adopters in the morning, I hoped a few dogs would get adopted before we had to make the move.

Finally, as my mind began to quiet down, I rolled over and took one last glace at the clock across the room before closing my eyes and falling asleep.

Three hours was hardly enough sleep to run on, but when the alarm went off at six I bolted out of bed and began getting ready to head to Atlanta. To my surprise, Eric and Abby were already busy in the kennel getting the morning chores done.

"Good morning," Eric smiled as he kissed me on the forehead.

"Morning," I replied, stifling a yawn. "What time did you guys get up?"

"Abby had me up about an hour ago. She said you didn't sleep well and that you would probably be tired this morning and she wanted to get a head start on all the work."

"How did you sleep? I asked, still feeling bad that he had traded his comfortable bed in for my couch.

"With one eye open. I can't wait to be moved out of here so we can all relax and not have to be constantly on edge."

"I agree with you there," I laughed. Following him out to the main kennel, we all finished passing out the dogs breakfast together before loading into the suburban to head for Atlanta.

I tried to avoid this particular shelter as much as possible since it was high kill. Every time I had been forced to come here, it was hard to leave without taking a handful of dogs with me. Today, I would be taking a lot more than a handful however.

The assistant director met us at the door and expressed her gratitude for us taking them in. "It's too bad we are unable to adopt them to the public, there are some really sweet dogs in that group. I'm just glad they will have a second chance at your facility."

Following her to the back of the building, she led the way through several sets of locked doors that had caution signs hung on them. Upon entering the last room, I saw rows of kennels filled with dogs.

"It's a good thing you came this morning," she yelled above the barking dogs. "We have had several cruelty cases come in the past week and are busting at the seams."

Looking around at all the dogs, the first thing I noticed was that they all appeared to be pit bulls. Leaving the woman behind, I wandered down the row and silently peered into all the kennels. The last few had 'Do Not Enter' signs posted on the gates and the kennels were padlocked shut. Reading the intake forms, it didn't take long to figure out that just about every dog in the room came from a fighting operation. There had to be over fifty dogs in here, and besides the ones we were taking, they would all be euthanized.

My stomach began to turn at the idea of all these lives lost, and the only reason they were here was because of the ignorance and greed of humans.

"Let's get the dogs loaded up," I told Eric. "I have to get out of here."

Leading the dogs out one at a time, we loaded them into crates once they were outside the facility. Thankfully the shelter had offered us the use of their van, and between that and the suburban we were able to transport all the dogs in one trip.

Once all the dogs were unloaded and settling into their new, temporary rooms, I dug though the adoption papers and borrowed Eric's phone to make a few calls to give the potential adopters a heads up that we would be moving within the week and if they wanted to follow through with the adoption it would have to be within the next couple of days.

There were two buses that I had set up appointments to look at later in the afternoon, so while we were waiting we began setting all the crates up in the play room. With the move coming up so quickly, we had to utilize every spare minute we had to get things ready.

"Can I ride with you?" Abby asked as we worked together setting up the last few crates.

"How about you switch between me and your dad, that way he has company on the ride as well?" I suggested. I had never gone on a long distance trip like this in a vehicle, but I could only image it to get boring behind the wheel alone for hours at a time.

"Sounds good to me," she chirped.

Before we knew it, everyone was loaded back up in the suburban and headed to look at the vans. I was used to my days flying by, but it seemed like there just wasn't enough hours in the day today to get everything done. Luckily the first one we looked at turned out to be perfect and we didn't even bother to look at the second one, leaving us a little extra time to stop and pick up some more crates since we were short by a few.

Eric set to work securing the crates in place and then began constructing a platform to put the smaller crates on above the large ones to make enough room for everyone to fit. The only thing left was to put up dividers so the dogs wouldn't be able to see each other and cause more stress on top of the long travel.

Monday morning came quickly, and once all the dogs were loaded into their crates, I had to stop and look around to let everything sink in. This was the last time I would ever step foot inside the facility that started it all. After taking one last walk through the kennel, I forced myself to close the door behind me as I left the place that had become my home.

Before climbing into the driver seat of the suburban, I did one last check to make sure everything was good in the van and gave Eric a quick kiss before we hit the road. As we pulled out of the drive way, I looked in the rearview mirror and watched as the warehouse disappeared out of view. Glancing over at Abby, I saw her studying me.

"Are you sad that you're leaving?" she asked.

Trying to stay strong, I smiled and told her that no matter how many memories we had gained here, it was nothing compared to what was coming.

ABOUT THE AUTHOR

Growing up in a small town in Michigan, Nicole didn't discover her passion for rescue until she began traveling with her family as they followed her father's job from state to state. While living in Pennsylvania, she found two puppies dumped on the side of the road and took them in. A year later while living in Alabama, she rescued her third dog from a high kill shelter. Upon moving back to Pennsylvania to take a job at a no kill animal sanctuary as a canine caretaker, her passion for rescue hit its all-time high. At that point she was hooked and the world of rescue took over. Since then, her main focus has been to open a rescue of her own, where she can rehabilitate as many dogs as possible and get them into loving homes.

24571488R00135

Made in the USA
Columbia, SC
24 August 2018